APPLEBY AND THE OSPREYS

An Inspector Appleby mystery

Clusters, a great country house, is troubled by bats, as Lord and Lady Osprey complain to their guests, who include first rate detective Sir John Appleby. In the matter of bats, Appleby is indifferent, but he is soon faced with a real challenge – the murder of Lord Osprey, stabbed with an ornate dagger in the library.

APPLEBY AND THE OSPREYS

APPLEBY AND THE OSPREYS

by

Michael Innes

Dales Large Print Books
Long Preston, North Yorkshire,
BD23 4ND, England.

British Library Cataloguing in Publication Data.

Innes, Michael
Appleby and the Ospreys.

A catalogue record of this book is
available from the British Library

ISBN   978-1-84262-631-3 pbk

Published in Large Print 2008 by arrangement with
A P Watt Ltd.

Dales Large Print is an imprint of Library Magna Books Ltd.

F

Printed and bound in Great Britain by
T.J. (International) Ltd., Cornwall, PL28 8RW

1

'Reflect, my dear,' Lord Osprey said to his wife. 'Or merely think. Better still, think *twice.*'

It was a mannerism of Lord Osprey's to be thus emphatic in his speech. One almost saw words and phrases in italic type as one listened to him. John Appleby, who along with his wife had just sat through a rather large luncheon-party given by the Ospreys, recalled how, one evening not long before, he had idly flicked a switch on a television set, and as a consequence found himself listening to his present host delivering a speech in the House of Lords. Not a maiden speech, or none of the scattering of peers present would have been so discourteous as to go to sleep. As it was, they had suffered Osprey through numerous sessions, and knew their man. So not only were some of them genuinely slumbering; here and there one of them – man or woman – was feigning slumber in the interest of providing more quiet fun for the BBC's cameras. It is proverbial that an Englishman loves a lord, and a gaggle of lords or ladies sleeping their way through parliamentary debates is probably more lovable still. Not – Appleby told himself – that they overdo the quaintness attaching to their labours as legislators. Only the Lord Chancellor on his woolsack is habitually addicted to fancy dress. And the woolsack itself – according to the high theory of the thing – is not inside but just outside their lordships' Chamber.

'Or for that matter,' said Lord Osprey, '*consult* Sir John.'

This was slightly awkward, since Appleby had failed to follow whatever topic the Ospreys were at issue over.

'I'm afraid,' Judith Appleby said, 'that my husband has withdrawn his attention and is thinking about Tom Thumb.'

This ought to have gone down well with Lord Osprey, since it was from an eminent statesman, Charles James Fox, while discoursing on Catiline's Conspiracy, that Dr Johnson had licensed his mind to wander to such odd effect. But Lord Osprey, who had certainly never heard of Catiline's Conspiracy, and hardly of Samuel Johnson either, was merely perplexed, so that a moment's silence succeeded.

'I would be so grateful for advice,' Lady Osprey then said unconvincingly. 'Bats in the belfry! And people being disturbed by it.'

'Yes, indeed,' Appleby said. 'One can only sympathize.' This was a reasonable shot in the dark. Perhaps Lady Osprey had been confiding to the company in the matter of some relative undeniably off his head.

'And you feel,' Judith asked quickly, 'a particular responsibility? As leading parishioners, that is to say.'

Appleby glanced at his wife in some alarm. Judith's sense of humour occasionally took a slightly malicious turn. And, after all, parishes do have leading parishioners. Particularly in the countryside. It can be made to sound comical, but is one of the facts of English rural life.

'Just so,' Lady Osprey said. 'And, indeed, a little more than simply that. Oliver, you see,' – Oliver was Lord Osprey's Christian name – 'is the vicar's churchwarden. And a very delightful old village shopkeeper is the incumbent's.' Lady Osprey paused on this, as if to mark its robustly democratic ring. 'So Oliver, and to some extent I myself, have a responsibility to give a lead in the matter. And, of course, Mr Brackley too. Mr Brackley is the incumbent. One couldn't have a more delightful parson than Mr Brackley. But he is sometimes a little slow when a decision has to be taken.'

'I think Brackley is quite right not to bother his head over anything so rubbishing.'

This came from a darkly frowning young man understood by Appleby to be the Ospreys' only son, the Honourable Adrian Osprey. (The Ospreys, although they had been barons through several centuries, had never contrived to yank themselves into an earldom – so Adrian, during his father's lifetime, was just a mere Hon. It was possible to wonder whether Adrian Osprey, whose temperament seemed to be distinctly saturnine, contrived to manufacture a grievance out of this lowly status.)

'So the matter of the bats in the belfry is a little hanging fire?' Appleby asked. He was now assured that the bats were actual bats, and not metaphorical ones in the head of some other difficult relative. 'The bats up there have become really troublesome?'

'It seems so,' Lady Osprey said. 'I am myself quite fond of bats in their proper place. We have them in the park, you know; and they have perfectly adequate roosting areas – if that's the proper term – in a disused barn at the home farm. In the dusk they come quite near to us here, and they particularly like the moat.' Lady Osprey paused on this, and it was clear that she conscientiously took satisfaction in the Ospreys' having such a mediaeval appurtenance to their dwelling. 'The moat has some quite deep pools in places, but in others it is simply rather soggy – and no doubts breeds the midges and things the bats feed on. Everything in its place, I say, and I don't even object to pic-nickers in the park if they keep their distance. But I feel that bats are not quite in their right place in churches. And in our church the creatures appear to wake up at the wrong time, and come down so that they frighten the village children in the choir. And the children are the choir. I don't know why it is – but there are now no grown-ups left in it.'

These rambling remarks failing to elicit comment from the guests at large, Lord Osprey had to take up the tale.

'At first it seemed simple enough,' he said. '*Bat* the belfry bats. Go after them as if they were so many deathwatch beetles. But then some confounded woman came and upset Brackley. Well-connected and so on, and from the Cruelty to Animals. I subscribe to them, as a matter of fact. So you might think they would leave us alone. But not a bit of it.

Bats, it seems, are a threatened species. Like badgers and foxes. It seems there would be no foxes left, if one didn't have hunts to go chasing and hallooing after them. I have to subscribe there too, you know, even although I don't at all regard myself as a landowner. A dozen farms to keep an eye on, of course. But you have to go back a good many generations to find any Ospreys as landed proprietors in a big way.'

Nobody in the small group of guests who had lingered to a civil three o'clock found any remark with which to follow up this genealogical information, so Judith Appleby returned firmly to the bats.

'There is a great deal of misconception about bats,' she said. 'Hardly anyone knows, for example, that they make excellent pets. Those village children ought to be told about that. A bat in a good home responds quickly to affection. And it doesn't need to be fed from expensive tins.'

'Very true,' an elderly woman called Miss Minnychip said. 'If the children ceased to be scared of them, the bats as they drop down at matins might join in the Benedicite. "O all ye Fowls of the Air, bless ye the Lord: praise him and magnify him for ever." Ananias, Azarias, and Misael oughtn't to be

14

left to do all the work.' Miss Minnychip reflected for a moment. 'And more simply,' she then added, 'recall that blessed are they that dwell in Thy house. The psalm explicitly mentions sparrows and swallows, but it says nothing about excluding bats.'

Not unnaturally, this speech occasioned general bewilderment. One or two people, realizing that Miss Minnychip had been quoting scripture, looked actively disapproving. Lord Osprey, although not perhaps a very observant man, did observe this and firmly wound up the topic.

'A tricky matter for Brackley,' he said. 'Either action or inaction is sure to offend some worthy people round about. Nevertheless something must be done, and with our authority behind it. I leave it to my wife, who sees more of our neighbours than I do. Only, she must *reflect;* must give her mind to it. Would anyone care to stroll through the gardens?'

This invitation was Lord Osprey's customary form of *au revoir,* and a sufficient number of his guests were aware of the fact for the party to break up at once. There wasn't, of course, a stampede. Everybody, that is to say, punctiliously murmured their regrets at being unable to accept so agreeable a suggestion, because of one pressing afternoon engagement or another; and the departure of the remaining guests in their cars fell decently short of a cavalcade.

'Roses,' Judith Appleby said as she took her place at the wheel of the ancient Rover. 'It would have been roses – and Lady Osprey would have known nothing about them.'

'She didn't seem to know much about bats either. Nor did her husband, for that matter. By the way, shall we take a look at the church? There it is, in a corner of the park. A convenient Sunday morning stroll from the big house in fine weather, and in foul no more than eight or nine minutes in a carriage. Inside, there will be a family pew for Ospreys, and three or four other pews hired for various grades of retainers.'

'I don't think it will be quite like that any longer. Very few of the retainers, as you call them, will think of themselves as obliged to go to church if they're to earn their keep. As for their children, those of them that sing in the choir – or that sing in the choir when not scared by an occasional bat – they no doubt have to have various treats and outings laid on for them. But let's take a look, as you suggest.'

2

The church proved to be – unlike Clusters, the ancestral seat of the Ospreys – unassuming and not in the best repair. Over the crossing there was a squat tower with crockets, and at the west end the belfry was a box-like structure with narrow unglazed lancets. Once inside, one had only to stand beneath the belfry and look upwards to see both the bell itself and a small colony of bats depending from the rafters.

'A breeding roost,' Judith said knowledgeably. 'And I rather think they're the greater horseshoe variety, which is distinctly uncommon in this part of the country.'

'Shall we give them a shout, or sing a hymn, and see what the effect is?'

'I'd rather you didn't, sir.'

This remark or remonstrance came from behind the Applebys, who turned round and saw at once that they were being addressed by the vicar, Mr Brackley. In the Anglican world a sense of trespass always attends upon being detected in a church other than

17

for devotional purposes at some prescribed hour. And if one's demeanour is in any degree frivolous or even merely cheerful one is apt to feel the impropriety of one's intrusion all the more keenly.

'I apologize,' Appleby said. 'My suggestions weren't very seriously intended. It so happens that my wife and I have been hearing about the belfry bats, and we thought we'd come and take a look.'

'Ah, yes! Yes, indeed. You have been visiting the Ospreys possibly? Excellent parishioners, but they have perhaps allowed themselves a shade too much concern about the harmless creatures. I am myself for a little delay, so that an undisturbed *accouchement* be achieved. Until their brood is born, that is to say. But perhaps I may introduce myself? I am Charles Brackley, the vicar of this parish.'

'Our name is Appleby,' Appleby said.

'Ah, yes! How do you do?' Mr Blackley turned to Judith. 'Lady Appleby,' he said, 'do you take an interest in bats?'

'I'm afraid I've never made a study of them,' Judith said. She was a good deal impressed by this deftness in identification. 'But I know one species from another. And it rather surprises me that this lot drop down in a disturbing way into the church –

18

and in daylight too. Normally, bats are surely the most crepuscular of creatures.'

'It is quite an infrequent performance, as a matter of fact. But some of the children find it alarming. What troubles them, I think, is the appearance the bats give of darting around in a helpless and aimless fashion. It is, of course, an appearance only. The truth of the matter is that they fly with a precision that astronauts might envy. Not a single one but has an inbuilt sonar system of the utmost delicacy. The direction, speed, distance of the smallest insect, they command through an ability to measure what to us are inconceivably minute fractions of time – and they communicate by a system of squeaks that few, if any, human ears are attuned to hear.'

'Nature in rather an elaborative mood,' Appleby said.

'It may be so regarded. But theologians, I believe, would account for all the endless diversity of created things by evoking the doctrine of what they call the Divine Abundance.' It was clear that the Reverend Charles Brackley didn't presume to reckon himself a theologian.

'I don't think I've heard of the Divine Abundance,' Judith said. 'Is it at all readily made intelligible?'

'I believe it is. God, having all eternity both behind him and in front of him, is always in danger of getting bored. So he occupies himself ceaselessly in thinking things up. Ceaselessly he creates diversity. But whether or not also for our instruction or entertainment, it would be hard to say.'

Thus edified, the Applebys made suitable remarks, and presently went on their way. And Appleby's mind reverted to Lord Osprey.

'So much for the Church's problem,' he said. 'But why should Osprey shove it – for what it's worth – at his wife? He's the churchwarden, not she.'

'Perhaps he has to think about Bills and Budgets and things.'

'Nonsense. The man's a legislative ignoramus. What do you imagine he does with his time? He has to fill it, I suppose. Rather like that parson's God.'

'I've heard that Lord Osprey has a hobby.'

'Judith, I sometimes wonder whether there's anything you *haven't* heard about anybody in this entire county.'

'It's simply because information, however useless, tends to stick in my head. Lord Osprey has a hobby. What could be more useless than knowing that?'

'One can never tell. It certainly isn't very startling information in itself. But perhaps the nature of the man's hobby is a little out of the way. Just what is it?'

'Numismatics.'

'He collects old coins? I do find that slightly odd. I imagine anybody with enough money, and with time on his hands, can form a collection of such things. But it's rather a learned field, I'd suppose – or is if one's going to get much satisfaction out of it. One has to be an ancient historian, and a more or less modern one too, to rank as any sort of numismatist. Does Osprey employ some harmless drudge as a curator or secretary or something?'

'Nothing of the kind. Osprey has a brother-in-law who provides the necessary erudition. He was there, as a matter of fact, but I suppose you weren't introduced to him. He was the man who sat in absolute silence next to Miss Minnychip. It seems his name is Marcus Broadwater. So Lady Osprey must have been a Broadwater. The family's not from this part of the world, and I don't know anything about them.'

'Do you know whether this learned Marcus Broadwater lives in the house?'

'Only off and on, probably. I think he's

some kind of rather peripheral Cambridge don.' Judith was silent for a moment as she negotiated a tricky turn in the narrow country road. 'Talk of the devil!' she then said. 'There he is.'

'Broadwater?'

'Yes, Broadwater. He has just crossed the road, and taken that field-path to the river.'

'An angler, it seems. And, presumably, a keen one, to have got into those togs and all this way from that boring lunch. He must have piscatorial as well as numismatic interests. And his brother-in-law probably owns the fishing rights for a good stretch of the river.'

'Broadwater certainly seems to expect a good catch. Look at the big basket he carries. And that sort of landing-net thing.' Judith appeared amused by the spectacle of so complete an angler. 'But, John, why do men who go fishing always wear deerstalker hats? It seems to mix things up.'

'It's to stick a good variety of their dry flies in, as you can see. All sports have their superstitions. Every seasoned angler believes that there is just one fly that the trout will currently go for, and that he has only to find it and cast it.'

'And cast it, I suppose, when he is himself

up to the knees in the stream. Did you notice his waders?' Judith had been much amused by this unexpected appearance. 'Shall we stop the car, and stroll after him, and make admiring noises when he catches anything?'

'Certainly not. Broadwater might very reasonably regard it as an impertinent intrusion.'

'Or we could talk to him about coins.' This suggestion being also unfavourably received, Judith drove on silently for some minutes. 'Coins,' she then said, 'must have rather the same sort of fascination for a collector as diamonds and emeralds and precious stones in general. Unlike pictures or statues or even books, they can be tucked away in a very small space and gloated over.'

'Infinite riches in a little room.'

'That kind of thing. And I have no doubt that a rare and very ancient coin can be worth enormously more than its original face value.'

'Most certainly – and there may be a special fascination in that. Do you think, Judith, that if we had been much more prestigious guests than we were – minor royalty, say, or something like that – we might have been invited to gloat?'

'It's possible. But – do you know? – I believe I've heard that Lord Osprey makes something of a mystery of where the collection is kept. It won't be in a kind of strong room with the pricier family silver. It will be somewhere more fanciful than that.'

'I doubt it. Osprey doesn't strike me as a fanciful type. In fact, my dear, you get these odd ideas as a kind of reflection from my long association with the more *recherché* kinds of crime.' Appleby fell silent for some minutes after this, and when he spoke again it was in what seemed a random and inconsequential way. 'I was a much better policeman, you know, than I am the country gentleman you've turned me into in my ripe old age.'

'You do hanker, John – don't you? And it isn't for your final eminence as the top bobby in London. It's for the position of the promising young man in the CID.'

'That's deplorably obvious, I'd say.'

'And it's why, every now and then, you still run into mysteries accidentally on purpose.'

'No doubt. But I don't think the Ospreys are a promising hunting ground. In fact they drop out of our lives here and now – until you decide it's time to ask them to lunch or dine.'

'One never knows,' Judith Appleby said.

One never does. Ten days later, and at an early hour, Appleby was called to the telephone.

'Detective-Inspector Ringwood speaking. Sir John Appleby?'

'Good morning, Mr Ringwood.' Appleby had repressed an impulse to say something like 'I ain't done nuffink', or even 'It's a fair cop. I done it, sure enough'.

'I'm deeply sorry to have to tell you, Sir John, that his lordship is dead.'

'What lordship? And why are you ringing me up about it?'

'As one of his close friends, Sir John.' The unknown Ringwood sounded cautiously reproachful. 'At Lady Osprey's urgent request, Sir John. She assures me you were that.'

'Lady Osprey overstates the case, Mr Ringwood. She could hardly overstate it more. If Lord Osprey has hanged himself, or been strangled by a demented butler, or anything of that sort, of course I'm sorry to hear of it. But I don't see that you have any occasion to communicate with me. Distraught women – or men, for that matter – frequently make senseless suggestions to the police. An officer of your experience, Mr Ringwood' – Appleby had decided that Ringwood was probably a decent copper but a little confused as well – 'must have come across that sort of thing often enough.'

'I don't know that I have, sir. But if you don't feel you have any concern in the matter, I must just apologize for troubling you.'

'There's no occasion for an apology, Mr Ringwood. What has actually happened?'

'Stabbed in the throat, Sir John. And killed outright. It's the way you might treat a pig, if you ask me.'

'I keep a few pigs, Mr Ringwood, to beguile the tedium of old age. But I haven't, as it happens, had to do my own slaughtering of them.'

'Of course not, Sir John. But it's right to tell you that Lady Osprey is much overwrought.'

'Naturally. But are you telling me merely that something horrible has occurred, or is it that an element of mystery is involved?

'Definitely a mystery. The perpetrator must be said to have left no clue.'

'Can you mean more, Mr Ringwood, than that, so far, you haven't found one?' This was an ungracious question, and Appleby repented of it at once. 'And Lady Osprey,' he continued, 'wants you – well, to consult with me in the matter?'

'It appears to be what is in her mind, Sir

John. And I would, of course, be very grateful–'

'I simply can't do anything of the kind. You
know that as well as I do. It's no less impossible than if I happened still to be Commissioner of Metropolitan Police.'

'Quite so, sir. I fully realize that. But the
lady also thinks of you as a personal friend
of the deceased, as I've said.'

'I tell you I am nothing of the kind. Just
something more than a nodding acquaintance. My wife and I, as it happens, lunched
with those people about a fortnight ago.
That kind of thing.'

'Am I to communicate to Lady Osprey
that you see it in that way, Sir John?'

'Certainly not.' Appleby thought for a
moment. 'It's a fair cop,' he said – and this
time it was aloud.

'Sir?'

'I mean that it will be only the decent
thing to turn up. To condole with Lady
Osprey, that is. Are you yourself, Mr
Ringwood, at Clusters now?'

'Yes, I am – and the police surgeon too. We
are in Lord Osprey's library, where the body
was found.'

'The venue must be said to be a little
lacking in originality, Mr Ringwood.'

'And, of course, there are those house-party people milling around.'

'Those *what?*'

'It's Lady Osprey's name for them. Week-end guests. There are half-a-dozen of them.'

'And the wretched people haven't had the decency to pack up and leave quietly?'

'I thought it best, Sir John, to ask them to stay on for a bit. They haven't all been too pleased. One of them – some sort of a high-up lawyer, he seems to be – asked me in a dry way whether he was supposed to be helping the police with their inquiries. I said it was just that, and he was quite amused by my reply. Amusement didn't seem to me altogether right in the circumstances'

'No more it was, Mr Ringwood. But go on.'

'Quickfall, his name is. Outlandish, it seems to me.'

'Rupert Quickfall, would it be?'

'Quite right, Sir John. You'd be knowing him, would you?'

'Only by reputation. I've never met him. But he's a QC flourishing at the criminal bar.'

'Well, Sir John, Mr Quickfall may find himself in a novel part of the court. But so may any of the others. So far, I must say I'm obliged to him. As things stand, I have no right to ask any of them to stay put for as much as half an hour. But Quickfall went round and persuaded them – or all except a brother of Lady Osprey's.'

'And you say Lord Osprey's body is staying put too?'

'Certainly, Sir John. Our doctor and the local GP have stirred it around a bit – but that's only to be expected. As I said, it's here in the library, which is where the thing seems to have happened. Except for Lady Osprey herself, I've allowed nobody to come in. But I can't yet answer for just what occurred earlier.'

'Obviously not. Are any other of Lord Osprey's relations in the picture?'

'The brother-in-law, Sir John.'

'Mr Broadwater. I know about him. Anybody else?'

'The heir, sir. Mr Adrian Osprey. No other relation, I think.'

'I see. Is there any suggestion, by the way, of something like burglary or theft being involved?'

'Nothing of the kind has been brought to my notice, Sir John. But it's early days yet. Lord Osprey may have come upon a burglar or thief, and lost his life as a result. But it doesn't seem very probable.'

'I suppose not. And I only ask, Inspector, because I happen to know that somewhere in Clusters there is – or was – what is almost certainly a very valuable collection of old coins. Thoroughly portable, it's likely to be. Very much more portable than mere bullion of the same value. That brother of Lady Osprey's, Mr Broadwater, will be able to tell you about the collection.'

'I'll make a note of it, Sir John. And old coins could be put on the market here and there and now and then without much risk of detection, I imagine. So it would be an attractive haul.'

'Perfectly true. But one further question, Inspector. Can you rule out, out of hand, Lord Osprey's having slit his own throat? In that event, of course, there would be no crime involved.'

'It's certainly no longer a crime to try to do away with oneself. Or to succeed, for that matter. But a criminal charge, sir, may lie against somebody who has facilitated or urged a suicidal act.'

'Deep water there, Inspector,' Appleby decided that he had underestimated Ringwood. The man he was speaking to was a competent officer.

'Not that we mayn't find ourselves in deep water of some other sort, sir. That moat: we may find ourselves dragging it.'

'That may well be. I'll be with you...' Appleby corrected himself. 'I'll be with Lady Osprey in twenty minutes.'

3

Strictly speaking, and *pace* Lady Osprey and
Ringwood, Clusters didn't have a moat at all.
The baronial dwelling, which century by
century had grown larger and larger through
random additions judged suitably imposing
in their day, now covered the greater part of
a small island in the middle of a small lake or
big pond. Contact with what may be termed
the mainland was achieved by substantial
causeways running respectively from the
main façade of the dwelling, and at the back
from various offices. Both causeways, although broad enough to admit of a couple of
carriages passing one another without hazard
on either side, were without rail or parapet,
but had been embellished from time to time
with chunks of masonry judged to be in the
mediaeval taste, including miniature bastions
from behind which equally miniature archers
might have operated. The lake or pond itself,
as if offended by this tomfoolery, had ab-
sented itself at least to the extent of shrinking
here and there into a condition of puddle or

mere sludge. In places, however, it remained quite deep, so that a small rowing boat maintained for the purpose could be potteringly propelled in a zigzag fashion to one or another vantage point from which guests of the Ospreys might view to the best advantage Clusters as a whole.

Why was the place called Clusters? The late Lord Osprey (as he must now be termed) had been fond of explaining that the original building was a monastery; that an ancestor of his had come by it at the time of the suppression and spoliation of such institutions in the sixteenth century; and that chance had preserved as *Clusters* what had been *cloisters* at an earlier period. Extensive cloisters, in fact, had been torn down – reprehensibly according to some ways of thinking – and Clusters had been built out of the abundant stone thus provided. Historians and philologists from time to time professed a certain scepticism about some of this, but no Osprey had been at all discomposed by them. Moreover, every Osprey knew about the family motto as it appeared cut in stone above an out-size fireplace in the mansion's billiard room. It was:

I prey

The charm of this was that it sounded pious, but that when you took a look at it a different sense appeared. If you happened to have preserved a Latin dictionary from your schooldays, and looked up *praeda,* you tumbled to the pun (or whatever it is to be called) at once. And the osprey, of course, is so named because it preys upon fish. It is pre-eminently the bird that does that. As Shakespeare's Aufidius tells us, it takes the fish by sovereignty of nature.

In the present set-up at Clusters it was a Broadwater, not an Osprey, who appeared to go after fish in a dedicated fashion. John Appleby – on his way, as he told himself, to condole with Lady Osprey on the untimely death of her husband – was made aware of this to a distinctly perplexing effect. As he approached Clusters, and close to the spot at which Judith and he had seen the man a few days before, he became aware of Lady Osprey's brother advancing towards him – and in his attire and all his piscatory para-phernalia he presented precisely the appear-ance that Appleby recalled from that pre-vious occasion. But what was striking now was the evident fact of Marcus Broadwater's proposing to indulge himself in his favourite sport hard upon the violent death of his brother-in-law. Angling is declared in a famous place to be the contemplative man's recreation, and conceivably Broadwater had decided that casting his fly at elusive trout might conduce to the state of mind required for – as it were – bringing the current mystery at Clusters successfully to dry land. But however that might be, there remained something distinctly odd in the man's thus deserting his own sister on what could scarcely be other than the most calamitous day of her life.

Upon the retired John Appleby this whiff of mystery had what was perhaps a predictable effect. He was moved to break in upon Broadwater's solitude forthwith, and to this end he brought his car to a halt immediately beside the field-path into which he guessed the fisherman would turn. When the man came within two or three yards of him he got out and spoke.

'Mr Broadwater, I think?' he said.

'You have the advantage of me, sir.' Broadwater's tone was distinctly chilly – but that, Appleby told himself, was fair enough from one who had been accosted in a most unwarrantable manner while going about his entirely peaceful occasions.

'My name is Appleby, and I was at that luncheon-party at Clusters a few days ago. I hadn't the pleasure of being introduced to you, but your identity was mentioned to me by my wife. She described you as the man who sat in absolute silence next to Miss Minnychip.'

This was far from polite, and presumably intended to be just that. There is much to be said for losing no time in irritating a witness. But if this was Appleby's proposal, it failed entirely. Broadwater's chilliness departed; he set his creel on the ground, leaned his rod casually across the bonnet of Appleby's car, and spoke with gentle amusement.

'Ah yes! Miss Minnychip. It is positively unkind to venture on a remark to her. She is one of nature's monologists, and conversation upsets her. You must have known people of that sort, Sir John. Some Home Secretaries, for example.'

Thus identified – as by Mr Brackley in his church – Appleby was obliged to fall back on civility.

'I must apologize for accosting you,' he said, 'on your way to what will be, no doubt, a capital day's sport. I've been told that, next after the Test, it's the best trout-stream in England.'

'It comes high on the list, certainly. We could talk about it for some time. A pleasant Curiosity of Fish and Fishing, you know.' Thus invoking Izaak Walton's ghost, Broadwater appeared to relax further. 'But, my dear Sir John, if you are interrupting me, isn't it correspondingly true that I am delaying you? For you are clearly hurrying to bring your professional skill to bear upon the circumstances of poor Oliver's death. Is it not so?'

'Your sister, Mr Broadwater, has sent a message asking me to come over to Clusters, and of course I have complied with her wish. I'll say what I can.'

Marcus Broadwater appeared amused by this evasive speech – as Appleby, indeed, felt the man was justified in being.

'Will it be only to my sister, Sir John, that you will say what you can? And not also to the fellow called, I think, Ringwood – who keeps on taking down what people say in a notebook?'

'I have never met Detective-Inspector Ringwood. But it was he who transmitted on the telephone your sister's invitation to me, and he struck me as a capable officer.' Appleby said this with some severity. 'And as

I am visiting Clusters anyway, it will perhaps be natural that he should have a word with me about this sad affair he has the duty of investigating. But I have no official standing in the matter at all, and I have no intention of poking around, solving a mystery, building up a case, or anything of the kind.'

'What a pity.'

'I beg your pardon?'

'The old war-horse neighs at the sound of the trumpet, does he not? I am inclined to think, Sir John, that my brother-in-law's sudden death may be an uncommonly seductive trumpet. And you have already responded to it, I may reasonably assert, by deferring your consolation of my sister in order to confront – shall we say to size up? – one promising suspect. He stands before you.'

'Mr Broadwater, you are now talking nonsense, or at least indulging in unseasonable whimsy. What your precise relations with your brother-in-law were, I don't know. But your sister has suffered a particularly painful and brutal bereavement, in the face of which levity – or an affectation of levity – ill becomes you. I think I had better drive on.'

'Come, come, my dear Sir John, don't be a prig. I don't know whether killing a brother-in-law rates as fratricide, but I do know that you will be quite wrong not to listen to a brief exposition of the manner in which something of that order may have occurred. I tell you I am a capital suspect. Are you, by the way, in the Queen's commission in this county?'

'If you are talking about being a JP – yes, I am.'

'Then is it not positively a dereliction of duty on your part not to listen to me?'

'I don't refuse to listen to you, Mr Broadwater. It was I who initiated our encounter, and I suppose I ought not to break it off.' Appleby realized that in this bizarre conversation he had been lured into something like a false position. 'If you really want to present a case against yourself, I must no doubt hear it – and pass on to Mr Ringwood whatever you have to say.'

'Capital, Sir John! I hope you will do exactly that. And I will begin by sketching what you have called my precise relationship to Oliver. I am a scholar by trade, and numismatics is my field of study. I pursue it at Cambridge, where I think I may say I am regarded as tolerably competent at my job. Oliver, who probably hoarded half-crowns and sixpences as a small boy, is now – or, rather, was until his death – the owner of a significant – and, of course, very valuable – collection of ancient coins.'

'Which you have been looking after for him?'

'I have been keeping the catalogue up to date, and advising upon acquisitions: that sort of thing. And I do a little cleaning from time to time. As you might imagine, that can quite often be a delicate operation.'

'I see. And where, Mr Broadwater, is the collection kept?'

'I have no idea.'

'My dear sir! That is a most extraordinary statement.'

'I am well aware of the fact. But even a large collection of coins can be tucked away in a very small space. The Osprey Collection, as it may be called, is just like that. Oliver simply wheeled it in.'

'Wheeled it in!'

'On a trolley. The kind of affair you see in restaurants for taking round the puddings and cheeses.'

'And you are telling me that, year after year, you have remained ignorant about the collection's normal place of security?'

'Just that. Or, at least, that's what I am asserting. But it will only be prudent not necessarily to believe anything I say.'

'You labour the point, Mr Broadwater. Would your sister have known where the coins were kept?'

'I much doubt it. I have never observed her take the slightest interest in the matter.'

'Are you going to claim that you had designs on the Osprey Collection; that you would have made off with it if you could?'

'Oh, most decidedly. And I'd have presented it to the appropriate museum at once.'

'And you ask me to believe that this situation is intimately related to the mystery of your brother-in-law's death?'

'Not quite that. I am merely outlining circumstances which must prompt you to place me firmly on your list – or on Ringwood's list – of suspected persons.'

'But does it, in fact, do that? I can see that, at times, Lord Osprey's secretiveness over his collection may have been extremely irritating to you. But is it in the least likely that, as a consequence of that irritation, you suddenly, and to no practical effect so far as the collection is concerned, stabbed the man to death in his own library?'

'That is very much the question, Sir John, to which I feel your Mr Ringwood should address himself.'

'He is not my Mr Ringwood. He is in a

sense, I suppose, your Chief Constable's Mr Ringwood.' Appleby paused on this, and saw that, although true, it was disingenuous as well. He must pull up on that insistent distancing himself from what could be called the Clusters Case. But he needn't pull up on thinking about Marcus Broadwater merely because the man had talked a certain amount of nonsense. Had he offered himself as a promising 'suspect' not as the consequence of more or less harmless eccentricity, but with some ulterior motive at present wholly obscure? Asking himself this, Appleby decided that it was time to end the encounter. 'A most interesting conversation,' he said. 'But to continue it further would be to keep you most unwarrantably from the trout. And I undertook to be with your sister nearly half an hour ago. So I must drive on.'

'Then good day to you for the present, Sir John.' And with some formality Broadwater doffed his deerstalker (at some hazard since it was so thick with dry flies) and, with a slightly ironical bow, picked up his rod and walked away.

Although he was already late for his appointment, Appleby found himself driving more slowly as Clusters came in view. Ahead of him was a man with his throat cut. And dead. He tried to remember whether just that had ever confronted him before. He had waged a long war against crime – and against the crime of murder often enough. But slit throats had somehow escaped him. Perhaps it was because his bosses had early taped him as the man to despatch when it had seemed a question of *recherché* crime. He had offered that phrase to Judith, he remembered, only a few days ago.

In the dictionary there was a singularly unpleasant word. *Jugulate.* To sever the blood vessels between heart and brain. In former days, when 'cut-throat' razors had abounded, suicides occasionally went about their task that way. Earlier still, when soldiers wore armour, the *coup de grâce* was sometimes delivered in the same manner: you pulled off a helmet and stabbed. Under any circumstances it was bound to be a pretty messy business. And there seemed to be a peculiarly bizarre incongruity in its happening in a library. Not that the library at Clusters was all that distinguished. At that lunch-party the guests had been offered a glass of sherry in it before going into a dining-room. It was the kind of library, Appleby had noted, that moved abruptly from eighteenth-century sermons to bound copies of *Punch* from 1841 onwards. A significant cultural shift, Appleby had reflected. So, for that matter, was the invention of the safety razor – which had perhaps been furthered by the career of Sweeney Todd, the demon barber of Fleet Street.

At this point in his wool-gathering Appleby became aware of a cyclist coming towards him. It was Mr Brackley, vicar of the bat-infested church. Brackley raised a hand as if in greeting – and then, as if on a second thought, rotated the hand in a manner suggesting a summons to stop. Appleby did so, and reversed a little. Brackley had dismounted.

'Good morning, Sir John,' he said. 'I think you must be making your way to the big house?' It was thus that Clusters must be spoken of locally.

'Yes, Mr Brackley, I am.'

'Then I think I ought to tell you–'

'Yes, I know. Osprey has met a violent death, and his wife has asked me to come over. The poor lady is under some absurd misapprehension about my position in these parts. She supposes me to be, not exactly its chief constable, but at least its Dupin or Mycroft Holmes.'

'Absurd, indeed.' Brackley spoke dryly. 'My own summons has been less idiosyncratic, but perhaps similarly tinged with oddity. I endeavoured to advance the comforts of religion, and I hope not wholly without effect. But the poor woman seemed to confuse me at times with the undertaker. Not that she isn't sensible and collected, after a fashion. There is to be a quiet burial here, witnessed only by the family, and later a memorial service in town, conducted by members of the higher clergy, and in the presence of numerous persons of quality.'

'That seems reasonable enough.' Appleby had been aware of a certain acrid quality in Brackley's speech. The Ospreys, he suspected, had been a little inclined to treat their vicar less as a beneficed clergyman than a domestic chaplain. 'There's something to be said for fixing one's mind on such matters when in a state of shock. And the shock must have been horrific. To have one's husband's throat slit in his own house! Think of it, Brackley.'

'Yes, indeed. The manner of the thing suggests a desperate malignity. Think of Laertes, Sir John.'

'Laertes?'

'Learning that Hamlet has killed his father,

he is prepared to cut his throat in the church.'

'It hasn't been quite like that – has it? Not a church, but a library. So not even bats to witness the thing.' Appleby was displeased at hearing himself produce this strained quip. 'By the way,' he continued abruptly, 'do you happen to know where Osprey kept that collection of coins?'

'I've no idea.' Brackley's features expressed surprise. 'But Lady Osprey's brother should know – Marcus Broadwater.'

'He doesn't – or he professes not to. I've just had an encounter with him, and I brought the matter up. He's gone off fishing.'

'Dear me! How slightly odd. Taking the thing, one may say, literally in his stride. I'm surprised the senior policeman up there – a fellow called Ringwood – let him go.'

'Ringwood could do no more than make a request, and he was backed by a barrister called Quickfall. I've gathered most of the house-party – for there has been a small house-party, as you must have noticed – have stayed put. But Broadwater collected his gear and went off.'

'Perhaps to think the thing out in solitude? Anglers, after all, are supposed to be given to meditating on the mutability of human affairs.' Brackley paused for a moment on this. 'Those coins,' he then said abruptly. 'Are you thinking that Lord Osprey's death may have followed upon a robbery or burglary?'

'It does seem to me a possibility. Clusters is, of course, full of what are called priceless things. But most of them are on the bulky side: Italian *cassoni*, full-length Van Dycks, and so on. Quite a large collection of coins could pretty well be carried off in a man's pockets. Are you interested in coins?'

This sharp question – part of a technique Appleby had commanded long ago – did take Brackley by surprise. But he answered easily enough.

'Oh, most decidedly! But not in the sense you intend, Sir John. On a vicar's stipend one has to take care of the pennies. Hence, for example, this bicycle. And I must speed home on it now. As you may imagine, there's rather a tricky sermon to concoct for this coming Sunday. Should you happen to be over here again then, it would be a great pleasure to see you in the congregation. And, meantime, please give Lady Appleby my regards.' Brackley swung a leg over his machine, and then appeared to have an after-thought. 'The butler up there might know something useful,' he said. 'He's an uncommonly knowing man. Name of Bagot.'

'I'll remember that,' Appleby said, and watched the Vicar of Little Clusters pedal away. Then he himself drove on.

4

Appleby was received by a tall and cadaverous man who was undoubtedly Bagot. Years had probably elapsed since the Ospreys had run to footmen. Bagot was dressed in ever so slightly greasy morning clothes. Like his betters, he would no doubt change into a dinner jacket when a bell rang in Clusters at seven o'clock. He carried a small silver salver on which he was presumably prepared to receive a visiting card if it was offered to him. Appleby asked for Lady Osprey.

'Certainly, Sir John. Her ladyship is in her sitting-room, and is expecting you. She relies upon you to clear up this horrible affair.'

Appleby might have come down on this like a brisk ton of bricks. He said nothing, however, and followed Bagot down long corridors oppressively hung with a jumble of small paintings and engravings and photographs which it was impossible to imagine anybody ever pausing to glance at. They were broad corridors, but seemed narrow because each as it was entered stretched into a middle distance as if situated in some vast ocean liner. Clusters really was an enormous place. Life, other than that of mice from the cellarage and midges from the moat, was confined to what was called the Georgian Wing, which was itself a very large mansion, confidently rather than arrogantly regardless of incongruity with the more modest achievements of Elizabethan and Jacobean builders. Looking for some scores of ancient coins in such a higgledy-piggledy museum would be – Appleby thought – as daunting an enterprise as setting sail in quest of the Golden Fleece.

The doors on the particular corridor down which he was now being conducted were of the duplex or bivalvular sort the ceremonious operation of which requires the regular attendance of a couple of lackeys at each. A practised hand, however, can make quite a show of the business on his own, and Bagot was accomplished at this. Without pausing in his measured pace, he thrust open both halves of such a door, stepped forward, said 'Sir John Appleby' in a subdued and almost casual tone. He then stepped aside to let Appleby past, reversed this movement, walked out backwards, and shut the door more or less on his nose. The low key of his announcement, Appleby concluded, had been designed to match the apartment into which he had introduced the visitor. It was large, but it wasn't at all grand. Lady Osprey's sitting-room – a term unassuming in itself – was furnished and equipped on what might be called a homely note. Appleby felt at once that he had discovered something about the social background of the Broadwaters. Marcus Broadwater was no doubt a highly cultivated Cambridge don, as well as a distinctly eccentric one. But neither he nor his sister belonged to what might be called the authentic Osprey world. Lady Osprey had developed a kind of patter which fitted Clusters after a fashion. But she had furnished this more or less private boudoir as something snug and nostalgic to retire to when thinking of simpler times.

'Dear Sir John, how kind of you to come. Do sit down.' Lady Osprey waved in an indicative manner at several chairs in quick succession. 'Poor Oliver – such a shocking thing! And quite unlooked for, too. I simply don't know where to turn. My brother Marcus is still with us, and he might be expected to take matters in hand a little. But Marcus has simply gone out to shoot things.'

'To fish things, Lady Osprey. I have just run into him fully equipped as a fisherman. But your son is at home, I take it, and must be a support to you in this very sad situation. May I say at once how much I feel for you. And my wife has asked me to say how grieved she is.' Appleby, who was genuinely sorry for this – as he felt – wholly unremarkable woman, got through these formal expressions without difficulty. He remained a little wary of Lady Osprey, all the same. It seemed not improbable that she would expect him to whip out a magnifying-glass and fall at once to scrutinizing the carpet with it, or something like that. 'But you have your son,' he repeated a shade hastily. 'He must be a great comfort to you.'

'But Adrian *knows* so little. And that is true, too, of the people now visiting us at Clusters. There is almost a house-party at present. Oliver, you know, liked that sort of thing. He was brought up to it. But that's true of Adrian too, I suppose. Yet Adrian doesn't like it a bit, either. His friends are in quite a different set, he says. It's an odd expression, and I think he must have picked it up from an old-fashioned novel. But I understand what it means. It means, among other things, that he will be barely civil to his parents' guests.' Lady Osprey managed a flash of spirit as she said this, but immediately afterwards her tone became plaintive again. 'Of course there is always Bagot,' she said. 'Bagot is a man who can be useful in all sorts of ways. But I have to confess I am always a little uneasy with Bagot. So, Sir John, I do very much hope that you can help me.'

'Anything I can appropriately do, I'll certainly do,' Appleby said – and at once felt that the speech had been unnecessarily wary: almost, indeed, ungracious. But at least it hadn't been unnecessary. Lady Osprey, he supposed, was firmly convinced that he was a kind of superior bobby who was happily in the neighbourhood at the right time, and the misconception must be cleared up at the start. 'Fortunately,' he went on, 'Detective-Inspector Ringwood appears to be a thoroughly able and conscientious–'

'Furniture-removers,' Lady Osprey interrupted. 'I am sure, Sir John, that you can help me there. It won't be a large undertaking, but some of the things are rather valuable, and a little fragile as well. And you know what most removal men are.'

John Appleby, who is not on record as

easily stupefied, came close to being so now.

'Do you mean,' he asked, 'that hard upon Lord Osprey's sudden death, you are giving thought to packing up and leaving Clusters?'

'Yes, indeed, Sir John. I have never liked this overgrown place – nor a lot that goes with it. All those dinner-parties and luncheon-parties and long weekends! Chatter, chatter about anything one can think of. Bats in the belfry, and heaven knows what.'

'And people bringing picnics into unsuitable parts of the park.' Appleby had now recovered himself. 'Do you intend to go far? It's long-distance removals, I take it, that can be rather tricky.'

'Only to the dower house.' Lady Osprey said this with a touch of grandeur: there was something to be said for a dower house, just as there was for a moat. 'The dower house, which is no more than a mile away, has of course been in the hands of tenants. But – most conveniently, isn't it? – their lease has just run out. Bagot – I've discussed it with Bagot – says that my moving there at once would be a little unusual. Because of Adrian's still being unmarried, he means. Unmarried eldest sons seldom want to have great houses all to themselves. Bagot says they usually have other ideas; that it would be much too much like settling down. One understands what he means.'

'Yes,' Appleby said. 'I suppose one does. Is Adrian fond of field sports: hunting and shooting and so on?'

'He certainly hunts. But hunting is something anybody can do anywhere – if he has the money, that is. And if, when I go away, he simply lets Clusters to an American millionaire, or somebody of that sort, he could no doubt reserve the fishing and shooting rights. I think that's the phrase.'

'Have you spoken to Adrian about your plan to move out, Lady Osprey?'

'No, not yet. I thought I'd leave it until after poor Oliver's funeral.'

'Which is when people will begin to address your son as Lord Osprey. There is much to be said for sticking to the proprieties in all these matters.'

Appleby was unsure whether he had offered this observation with any inflexion of irony. Certainly Lady Osprey's mind appeared to be behaving oddly – if not positively improper – in the context of the immediate state of affairs at Clusters. Fleetingly, Appleby wondered whether she was in a condition of such deep shock that she scarcely knew what she was talking about. But there was no real indication of anything of the kind. She disliked the place; an event had now happened which presumably caused her to dislike it even more; she was in a position to leave, and that was what she was going to do.

Or this – Appleby told himself – was the appearance of the matter. But about his whole encounter with Lady Osprey was there not more than a hint of oddity – almost of implausibility? Had he really been begged to come to Clusters only to find himself asked for advice about furniture removers – a subject which until now the lady hadn't with any tenacity pursued? And there was surely something grotesque in her almost totally ignoring the element of mystery surrounding her husband's horrible death. Quite suddenly, Appleby found himself wondering whether this seemingly artless person was in fact playing rather a deep game; presenting, for some end of her own, a kind of additional or subsidiary puzzle to a man who had been rising to puzzles through a long professional career. There was at least something disturbing in the notion that there existed, so to speak, more than one angler in the Broadwater family.

'I do hope you will stay to lunch with us,'

Lady Osprey said. 'You could have a chat with Adrian. And everybody seems to be staying at least till the afternoon. The policeman, I am told, was anxious they should do that in order that he could take statements from them.'

'Thank you: I shall be delighted,' Appleby replied – not, perhaps, without a certain sense of having taken the hook in his gullet. 'And now I ought to have a word with that policeman, simply in a friendly way. I haven't met him, but when he gave me your message on the telephone he sounded a sensible man.'

'But with an odd name. Ringworm, or something of the sort. And I'm afraid Adrian was rather rude to him. So be as nice to Mr Ringworm as you can.'

Appleby failed to take this injunction kindly, but refrained from revealing the fact. Lady Osprey rang a bell, and Bagot answered it so promptly that it was difficult to believe he hadn't been listening at the door. Had he in fact been committing this improbable impropriety, Appleby reflected, he would have learnt little that he didn't already know.

5

Detective-Inspector Ringwood had established himself – by this time with a considerable entourage – in the Music Saloon.

The Music Saloon was much the largest and grandest room in Clusters. Except when the Ospreys gave a ball (which was about once in a generation) hardly anybody ever entered it except persons armed with ladders and mops and vacuum cleaners. The lofty ceiling dripped enormous chandeliers; vistas of equally enormous mirrors suggested Versailles; at regular intervals between these rose Corinthian columns which, being unfortunately too plump even for their considerable height, were evocative less of Greece than of Pharaonic Egypt. There was a chimneypiece so elaborately (if inappropriately) besculptured with mermaids and tritons that it invariably formed the frontispiece of every book about chimneypieces to be published. There was also, in a rather deep recess between two of the wodgy columns, the celebrated *trompe-l'œil* door.

Visitors were indeed sometimes admitted to the Saloon to take a peep at this. The door had a harp perched against it, but the point a conducting Lord Osprey had to make was, of course, that the harp wasn't a real harp nor the door a real door; what one was looking at was nothing but paint skilfully applied to canvas. The late peer had been fond of explaining that the dodge had been copied at the Duke of Devonshire's Chatsworth, although there were books absurdly asserting that the borrowing had been the other way round.

The Music Saloon was also provided with a large platform for an orchestra, and it was on this that Ringwood – who, Appleby judged, must have a whimsical streak in him – had located the small assemblage of officers, male and female, which now, it is claimed, constitute a Murder Squad in all properly developed English constabularies. There weren't at all *trompe-l'œil:* there they solidly were, complete with wireless telephones, electric typewriters, cameras, and the computers that have become so indispensable in the fight against crime.

Appleby took this in respectfully enough, but as he shook hands with the Detective-Inspector he murmured something about finding somewhere for a quiet talk.

'We'll go to the library, Sir John,' Ring-wood said. 'You'll want to view the body.'

Appleby, in fact, didn't want to view the body. He had viewed plenty of bodies in his time, and had no inclination to add that of the late Lord Osprey to the list.

'I think not,' he said. 'If the thing came to a murder trial, and it became known that I'd had a sniff at the corpse, I might find myself under subpoena as a witness for the defence, or something of that kind. It wouldn't do, Mr Ringwood. It wouldn't do at all.'

'I'll just ring through to the men in the library, sir.' Ringwood was by now fully aware of his distinguished colleague's instinct for evasive action. 'If the photographers have finished their job, the corpse may already have been taken away to our mortuary. You wouldn't mind having a look at the room itself?'

'Not in the least. As it happens, I was in it a few days ago, drinking sherry. But I didn't take much account of it. The only thing I remember is a strong impression that the Ospreys as a family have seldom been very bookishly inclined. So telephone away.'

And Ringwood telephoned – not without betraying some satisfaction in the up-to-date contraption enabling him to do so. Then he turned back to Appleby.

'As I thought,' he said. 'Taken away ten minutes ago. The *corpus delicti*, as they say. I suppose it may have to be brought back later, to some sort of family vault or mausoleum. You'd expect an outfit like Clusters to run to something of that kind.'

'No doubt that's so.' Appleby rather approved of Ringwood's thus reaching for a more familiar note. 'It's only the rude forefathers of the hamlet who are likely to be buried in Mr Brackley's churchyard. Not that the little church doesn't run to a few storied urns – and even animated busts. But not, I think, to capacious tombs. No doubt Clusters has, as you suggest, its own provision of that sort of thing on or near the premises. Bagot will know. And I have a feeling that Bagot knows a good deal.'

So the men made their way to the library, amiably conversing as they covered the considerable distance this entailed. They found a couple of constables still on guard there. They looked at some coagulated blood on a rug. They looked round the large apartment as a whole. Appleby did his best to bring a fresh eye to the job, but was for the moment only confirmed in his impression that through a good many generations the pleasures of scholarship had eluded the Ospreys. And Ringwood, for his part, seemed positively depressed by the place.

'What you might call uncommunicative, isn't it?' he said. 'A necessary adjunct of what they term a stately home. But not really loved by anybody.'

'The window at the end there has a curious view. A narrow terrace and then what they call the moat. Slightly Venetian in effect, you might say. It might be some magnifico's water-gate.' Appleby paused on this remark, frowning as if displeased at its inconsequence. 'Is there any notion yet of approximately when the wretched man was killed?'

'The doctor's first impression is very late last night – even, perhaps, in the small hours. He says the top forensic man who's now on his way to us may come out with something more confident and definite. But he added that the fellow is paid to do just that.'

'I see.' Appleby was non-committal before this slightly unseemly scepticism. 'What about the weapon?'

'Probably quite a sizeable affair, he says. Not all that sharp, but distinctly up to its job. My men have carried out a pretty thorough search already, and have found nothing. The killer must have carried it away with him. Perhaps he chucked it in the moat. I don't envy the fellows who'll have to hunt there. About as mucky a job as you could imagine.'

'Yes, indeed.' Appleby glanced round the room. 'What about the space behind all those rows of books?'

'Those, of course. I'll have every volume shoved hard back to the panel behind it.'

'That for a start.' Appleby was silent for a moment. 'It might be better to have them out, shelf by shelf. If you have the man-power, that's to say.'

'Of course I have the man-power, and I'll do as you suggest.' If Ringwood was offended by this virtual instruction, he didn't show it.

'You know, it's odd what one sometimes doesn't see. Did you ever read a yarn by Edgar Allan Poe called *The Purloined Letter?*'

'I can't say I have, Sir John.'

'It turns on the notion that when one is hunting for what one believes to have been *concealed* one tends to stare straight through what has *not* been concealed. The letter is there under the searchers' noses, stuck – if I remember correctly – "in a trumpery filigree card-rack".'

'You couldn't very well stick a sizeable dagger or the like in a card-rack.'

'What about those trophies, Mr Ring-wood?'

'Trophies, Sir John?' If the word conveyed anything to the Detective-Inspector, it was perhaps to be applied to cups or mugs or jugs handed out at the close of an athletic occasion.

'The name is given, I think, to the sort of large-scale decorative arrangement of weapons and armour you see there on either side of the chimneypiece. Spears from the Zulu wars, the helmets of Roman legionaries dug out of the clay, dandified stilettos from the *seicento*, muskets once discharged against the armies of Napoleon, bayonets and hand-grenades from Flanders: the lot. And all radiating in a symmetrical design from a hub purporting to be nothing less than the shield of a Greek hoplite or a Japanese samurai. The idea is that your ancestors have been a martial crowd ever since they tumbled out of Noah's ark. And disposed as they are here in a library, the weapons assert that an aristo-crat has better things to do than learn his ABC.'

It is to the credit of Detective-Inspector Ringwood that he listened to this unusual flood of eloquence on Sir John Appleby's part with attention and respect.

'So you think,' he asked, 'that our murderer simply snatched one of those museum pieces from the wall, went to work with it, and then simply put it back in place again?'

'It's just a possibility, Mr Ringwood.'

'And if we take down the whole lot we'll find freshly congealed blood on one weapon or another?'

'That would possibly be so. The blood group would then be determined: all that. And what else would follow?'

'Quite a lot.' Ringwood spoke slowly, like a man finding his way on unfamiliar ground. 'The murder of Lord Osprey becomes unpremeditated, and a matter of imaginative resource and quick thinking as well. There's also a kind of gambling element in it or – or something almost taunting, crying "Catch me if you can".'

'Just that.' John Appleby knew how to be briskly approving. 'It couldn't be better put, Ringwood. And if we're right, if we find Osprey's blood on a blade, we have something like a psychological sketch of the man – the man or woman – who wielded it.'

6

Ringwood now took himself off to what he thought of as his headquarters in the Music Saloon, and as he did so he also withdrew the two guardian constables to the corridor outside the library. By this manoeuvre he contrived to leave Lady Osprey's visitor (who just happened to be a policeman too, although on the retired list) alone in the room in which, only a few hours earlier, Lord Osprey had been killed. This was quite a stroke on the Detective-Inspector's part towards implicating Sir John Appleby in the investigation of what was in itself an invitingly mysterious affair.

It wasn't, Appleby felt, an investigation that had made a great deal of headway so far. He had himself hit upon where the weapon might be found, but this was no more than a conjecture which had yet to be verified. And even if it was so verified, the motive prompting its use was still totally obscure. Who had murdered Lord Osprey, and why?

The only answer afforded to either of these

questions to date had been in the form of an eccentric and almost burlesque confession by the dead man's brother-in-law. Appleby found himself disliking Marcus Broadwater, but this dislike arose merely from his feeling that murder was never something to be funny about. Nor had Broadwater, in fact, offered a confession in any exact sense. He had merely obtruded himself as being a promising suspect in the affair, and had hauled in the elusive Osprey Collection of coins by way of motivating his supposed crime. There was surely a streak of sheer nonsense in this. Broadwater had professed himself ignorant of where the collection was kept; and if Lord Osprey was alone in possession of this secret, cutting his throat was by no means a good way of getting at it.

Broadwater was not to be eliminated, all the same. He might have advanced a wholly implausible motive for killing his brother-in-law by way of getting himself dismissed as a harmless eccentric when in fact he was nothing of the sort and had killed Osprey for some totally different reason.

Appleby paced moodily round the library. Why, near midnight or in the small hours, had Osprey been here at all? It could hardly have been to edify himself by reading eighteenth-century sermons or to shed his cares by chuckling over back numbers of *Punch*. Had he a known habit of nocturnal prowling through this vast travesty of a dwelling place? Was it conceivable that he occasionally kept disreputable trysts in this unfrequented apartment?

Appleby paused at the window through which – as he had idly remarked to Ringwood – there was an almost Venetian effect. It was a French window, beyond which was a small patch of paving, surrounded on its other sides by the area of stagnant water they called the moat. So it was just possible to imagine moonlight, and a courtesan stepping swiftly from a gondola into the arms of an expectant grandee waiting within the shadow of his palazzo. Something of this silly fancy – Appleby recalled with discomfort – he had actually offered to Ringwood. Into any such picture Lord Osprey didn't seem to fit at all well, anyway.

And now this unprofitable reverie on Appleby's part was interrupted by the sound of a considerable altercation in the corridor outside the library.

'I tell you I'm the owner of this whole bloody dump, and I'll go where I like in it!'

The door had been flung open, and now a young man burst into the library. He was followed by a red-faced constable who gave every appearance of having been thumped violently in the chest, and of being minded to do something thoroughly effective in reply.

Appleby strode rapidly across the room.

'All right, officer,' he said. 'Perhaps Mr Osprey and I can usefully have a quiet talk. But one of you get back to that Music Saloon and report the fact to the Detective-Inspector.'

This, of course, marked a further stage in Sir John Appleby's admitting involvement in the Osprey affair. The constable, relieved rather than perplexed, took himself off as instructed, and Appleby turned to Adrian Osprey.

'Are you, perhaps, looking for me?' he asked.

'Certainly I am. And it's to ask you what the devil you are doing here. And to tell you to clear out.'

'I am here on the invitation of your mother, sir. But I must add that, having once had some part in criminal investigation myself, I have felt bound to give Detective-Inspector Ringwood any assistance and advice that I can.'

It was thus that Appleby (who had only been up to his ankles so far) definitely crossed his Rubicon into the Clusters mystery. But who was his adversary; who, so to speak, his Pompey? Could it conceivably be the young man who had thus rudely burst in on him, and who was the heir to the whole place?

But Adrian Osprey now changed his note abruptly. He wasn't exactly polite. Politeness was perhaps something he simply didn't go in for. At a pinch he could manage civility, and it was this that he turned on.

'All right,' he said. 'I withdraw. About, I mean, ordering you to withdraw. I've heard, Sir John, that you've been a dab hand at this sort of thing in your time. So stay on. Stay the night, if you've a mind to it. I'll tell Bagot, or the housekeeper or somebody, to find you a room. We could put up the whole of Scotland Yard in this warren of a place without noticing it. Except, perhaps, by the smell. Sorry. Remarks of that sort are rather my thing.'

'It is a disadvantageous proclivity, sir, so far as any sort of career is concerned. You would do well to go after wit of a less offensive sort.' Appleby said this with the instant authority of a very senior man. 'As for staying the night, I am, of course, grateful for your offer of hospitality. But I am unlikely to have to avail myself of it. What is mysterious about your father's death is likely to be resolved quite soon. Contrary, no doubt, to popular belief, it is so with the majority of crimes.

Not unnaturally, this speech disconcerted Adrian.

'You mean,' he demanded, 'that this beastly murder of my father will be cleared up *today?* Why, that fellow Ringwood in the Music Saloon seems determined to set up a kind of permanent secretariat. It's as if he were going to be here till Christmas.'

'For a good many years I was much involved in that sort of approach myself. Shall we sit down?'

'Sorry, again.' Adrian Osprey grabbed a chair and thrust it at Appleby. 'My mother does a lot of fussing about getting people a pew. So I come rather short on it.' With this handsome apology, the heir of Clusters sat down too. 'But you gave it up? The sort of circus, I mean, that this chap Ringwood carries round with him.'

'It gave me up. I retired – so now I have to rely simply on the little grey cells.'

'Cells?' It appeared that Adrian was puzzled by this. 'Locking people up in quod?'

'I have been involved in a certain amount of that too.' The young man, Appleby saw, had the true Osprey innocence of the pleasures of literature, even in one of its lighter manifestations. 'But don't,' he said, 'underestimate Ringwood's regiment. The fingerprint wallahs, for instance. It's my bet that they'll arrive any time now in a big way. They'll dust through this whole room pretty thoroughly. Incidentally, they'll certainly want *your* fingerprints. And, I suppose, mine too.'

'Why ever should they do that?' It was in something like alarm that Adrian asked this question. 'I don't see—'

'Simply to eliminate us, my dear young man. As it's so evident that neither of us murdered your father, they'll want to ignore our fingerprints wherever they turn up.'

'Yes, of course.' It was perhaps a shade suspiciously that Adrian glanced at Appleby for a moment. Then he laughed abruptly. 'They'll have a job,' he said. 'All those bloody books, for instance! I doubt whether they'll turn out to be what are called well-thumbed volumes.'

Appleby received this joke with concurring jocularity. It was the first indication, he reflected, that the new Lord Osprey might have a streak of cleverness in him. And the momentary relaxation ought to be seized upon.

'Would you mind,' he asked, 'if I put a few questions to you?'

'Not a bit.' And Adrian sat back in his chair. 'Fire away, Sir John.'

'I don't doubt that you are a pretty observant young man. So what I'd ask first is whether – over, say, the last few days – you have been aware of anything out of the way going on here at Clusters?'

'I'd say not.' Adrian's features at once took on a look of pronounced perspicacity. 'It wouldn't be too much to say that nothing out of the way ever does take place at Clusters. It would be dead against the grain of the place, you know. It's why I don't spend much time in the old home. Home, sweet home, of course. But damned dull. Dull as ditchwater. Or as that bloody moat.'

'But you intend to change that a bit? As the new owner, I mean.'

'It would be an uphill job, Sir John. And I don't know that I intend, just because my father has gone, to plant my bottom any more frequently in the family seat. Peers, of course, do have seats. It's undeniable. The country seat of the young Lord Osprey! Balls to it.'

This was clearly a dismissive remark, and Appleby moved on.

'I am thinking, in particular, of the past twenty-four hours. Nothing occurred in them that strikes you as worth mentioning?'

'Nothing at all. Or only the business of the lurking intruder, I suppose. You'd have to ask Jane Minnychip about that. The old cat came to dinner, you know. And, because of the fuss Ringwood is making about coming and going, she's here still.'

'I remember Miss Minnychip. Tell me about her, please.'

'She's a useful guest, who lives not far away. In a little house a couple of miles from what we call the dower house. Yesterday my mother found she'd muddled our dinner party – as she often does. We were a woman short, so the chaste Jane was summoned at short notice. She often is. And because the short notice is a bit against the polite rule book in such matters, she's always asked to stay the night. That's why she's here still. Because of that, and then because of this Ringwood's wanting everybody to stop on for a bit. The whole rotten little house-party is in a sort of deep freeze. All, that is, except my uncle Marcus. He's gone fishing.'

'I know he has. I met him on his way, and we had a word together. But go on telling me about Miss Minnychip and the lurking intruder.'

'It's really about my father and the lurking intruder. But *he* can't tell you, and *she* did have a glimpse. We were all, or nearly all, in this room, drinking that eternal sherry. It was already dusk, of course, and the lights were on, but nobody had closed the curtains on that big French window. It was something, you see, that my father rather liked to do himself. He liked to stare out at that glorified puddle of ours in the dusk, probably taking satisfaction in thinking about generations of Ospreys having done the same thing. Which was rot, anyway. There's nothing mediaeval or Tudor or what have you in this whole part of the dump. It's what they call late Georgian. Somewhere or other there's a date carved on it. 1815, I think.'

'A notable year.'

'Is it? I wouldn't know. I don't much care for history.'

'And history may conceivably return the compliment. But go on. We've got to your father liking to close those curtains himself.

He did so last night.'

'Yes – but not without this odd spot of brouhaha.'

'Of what? But never mind. Go on.'

'He'd put out his hand to that tassel-thing you pull down to do the job. And the Minny-chip was following him, jabbering. She's that sort of female.'

'No doubt. But then?'

'My father – who has been a bit nervy of late – gave an odd sort of exclamation. It might have been of mere surprise, or it might have been of straight funk. And the Minny-chip let off a yelp of her own. Between them they may be said rather to have startled the nobility and gentry waiting to be fed. Only my Uncle Marcus – Marcus Broadwater, you know – made a dash for the window. Marcus is only a bloody Cambridge don, but he does have some guts to him. My father, however, had given a vigorous tug, and the curtains took the hint. End of episode. Or not quite. My father turned and said, "Some damned intruder out there", and the Minny-chip chirped, "I had a glimpse of him, too." She seemed to feel that she'd distinguished herself.'

'Was there an immediate investigation?'

'Lord, yes. Quite a fuss for a time. Bagot

was going round with a decanter, topping people up with that tepid muck. My father told him to put it down, and go and investigate. Dear old Daddy was in a regular stew.'

'Frightened, you mean?'

'Just that. The Osprey blood in me was quite ashamed of him.'

'And just how could Bagot have investigated?' Appleby had walked over to the window and glanced through it. 'There's nothing out there except an odd sort of platform, and then the moat. Did Bagot part the curtains again and go outside?'

'No, he didn't. He was probably in a tizzy himself. He just bolted from the room – and came back after a time to say nothing had been discovered. Meanwhile, my father had come to his senses and played the thing down. He had several guests, you know, and I suppose he felt he was in danger of acting the poltroon before them. Rather a good word, poltroon.'

'Just what did he *say?*'

'He said he must have made a mistake. I don't think he believed he had. But then we all went in to dinner.'

'Has Ringwood been told about this? It's possibly highly significant.'

'I haven't a clue, Sir John. I certainly didn't

tell him myself.'

'Then you ought to have.' Appleby snapped this out. 'I must see Miss Minnychip. She may have noticed whether the intruder, as she glimpsed him, appeared wringing wet. He could only have swum, or waded, across the moat. Or is there a boat?'

'There's certainly a small boat that people plouter about in. It's kept in a shed on the other side of the moat.'

'It must be examined at once. Thank you for telling me about it.' And Appleby called in one of the constables and left the library.

Back in the Music Saloon, he found Ringwood in conversation with a lady. But this is a somewhat neutral and uninformative description of what was going forward. The lady was Miss Jane Minnychip, and she was haranguing a Ringwood who, if not positively discomfited, was visibly nearer to that condition than was at all seemly in a senior officer of the police. Nor was Ringwood's small cohort on the platform at the end of the room – although, doubtless, entirely in command of the computers and other gadgetry they had brought along with them – at all qualified to advance and support their commanding officer in an altercation with an indignant and vociferous gentle-woman. So the Detective-Inspector hailed Appleby with the mingled relief and deference which a hard-pressed field-commander might accord to a general turning up in a timely way at the head of something like an entire imperial guard.

'Sir John,' he said, 'this is Miss Minnychip, one of Lord Osprey's – of Lady Osprey's, I ought to say – guests. Miss Minnychip lives in the next parish. And she is asking – demanding might express it better – police protection for herself and her property. But what the reason is, I just haven't been able to get hold of. It's almost as if she is apprehensive of suffering the same fate as Lord Osprey, and on similar grounds – whatever those grounds may be. Miss Minnychip' – and Ringwood turned to the lady – 'is that what you are saying? And perhaps you can make the matter clearer to Sir John than to me.'

'I don't doubt I can,' Miss Minnychip said. 'And much more appropriately. Sir John, good morning. Mr Ringwood, you may withdraw.'

To this sudden assumption of grandeur the Detective-Inspector might have been expected to produce some distinctly crisp rejoinder, but at the ghost of a nod from Appleby he did turn to leave the room. And Appleby spoke at once.

'Miss Minnychip, may I tax your patience by speaking for a couple of minutes to Mr Ringwood?' Then, without waiting for a reply, he followed Ringwood from the room, and shut the door behind him. 'An odd piece of information,' he then said, 'which may turn out to be important. It seems that there is a little boat kept in a shed some-where on the other side of the moat. Have it found, will you? What we want to know is whether there are any signs that it has been in the water quite recently. I'll explain later. At the moment, I'd better not keep that woman waiting. She may have something important to say.'

And with this, Appleby returned to the Music Saloon.

7

'My dear Miss Minnychip,' Appleby said soothingly. 'I will, of course, be most happy to give you any help I can. But is your communication to be regarded as of a confidential sort?'

'Most certainly it is.'

'It has been my experience,' Appleby went on more weightily, 'that walls have ears – and particularly so where there has been any unfortunate affair, such as here at Clusters. So may I suggest that you and I take a walk through the gardens? Lady Osprey's roses are always worth looking at, are they not?'

This proposal commended itself to Miss Minnychip at once, and to the gardens the two accordingly made their way. The rose garden, in particular, afforded an admirable setting for private talk. It occupied a substantial part of the island site not taken up by Clusters itself, and when near the centre of it they could not be approached unobserved by anything bulkier than a pigeon or squirrel. Thus secluded, Miss Minnychip spoke at once, and to a mildly surprising effect.

'My late father,' Miss Minnychip said, 'collected ancient coins. And his collection is with me in my small house now.'

'I see. So your father and Lord Osprey were, in fact, fellow collectors. Did they hold much communication with one another over this interesting pursuit?'

'Lord Osprey came, of course, very much later into the field, and my father did advise him from time to time. And I can recall my father, in the very last year of his life, occasionally comparing notes with Lord Osprey's brother-in-law.'

'With Mr Broadwater? But of course.'

'Lord Osprey, I need scarcely tell you, was a much wealthier man than my father. But his interest in numismatics was not of any well-informed sort. It was, indeed, little more than a rich man's whim, and I think it may have been instigated in the first place by Marcus Broadwater himself. Mr Broadwater is a scholar – and my father, Sir Philip Minnychip, included scholarship among his many distinctions. My father, as a young man, had risen rapidly in the Indian Civil Service. Its members, unlike the army people, were, more often than not, persons who had pursued classical studies at school and university, and were of wide cultivation in general. It is a fact you yourself may be unaware of.'

'Not at all,' Appleby said. 'I am old enough to remember the high esteem in which the ICS was held.'

'Quite so. My father, upon his retirement, was awarded the KCSI. He may well be styled a man of many talents.' Miss Minny-chip paused on this, as if debating whether to embark upon the wealth of scriptural reference which Appleby recalled her as being addicted to. But on this occasion she kept to the point. 'Not unnaturally, my father had interested himself in the main in the coinages of the Orient. It is in that department of the subject that his own small collection is, I understand, of considerable importance. And let me say at once that the collection is small if compared with that of Lord Osprey. It is of very substantial monetary value now, nevertheless. Since my father's death the value of such things in the salerooms has shot up in an astonishing fashion. But fortunately my own circum-stances, although straitened, have never obliged me to think of parting with my father's collection in that way. I hope that it may eventually go to the Ashmolean Museum in Oxford. My father was an Eton and Christ Church man.'

'Was he, indeed?' Appleby said respectfully, and paused to sniff at a rose. 'But just how, Miss Minnychip, does all this affect our present situation?'

Asked this question, Miss Minnychip was silent for a moment. It could be felt as a disapproving silence, as if the answer to it were so evident that it ought not to have been put to her.

'We surely know,' she then said, 'that poor Lord Osprey has been done to death by desperate thieves who he came upon when they were attempting to make off with his collection?'

'It is one conceivable theory, certainly,' Appleby said. 'Yes, I think you have hit upon something distinctly possible. In fact, I must congratulate you on putting it forward. I hadn't thought of it. I don't believe that Ringwood has thought of it either. And I must confess that I've myself been thinking of something rather different.'

Miss Minnychip received this disingenuous speech with suspicion – as indeed she was abundantly entitled to do. Appleby hoped that her response stopped short there.

Even a retired Commissioner of Metropolitan Police, dragged into a thoroughly messy business, ought not to give way to an impulse of sheer mischief. Nevertheless it was on this reprehensible note that Appleby lingered for a further moment.

'What would you say,' he asked, 'about the possibility of its having been, on the contrary, a hideous domestic crime?'

'A what?'

'A hideous domestic crime, Miss Minnychip. They do happen, do they not? Even in the Bible. The ball was sent rolling when Cain killed Abel. And in modern times psychologists have had much to say about patricide, matricide, uxoricide, fratricide, infanticide, and so on. Again, some of the greatest modern novels turn on that kind of thing. For example, *The Brothers Karamazov*—'

'Sir John, pray cease from inappropriate levity.' Miss Minnychip, having thus found her bearings, was suddenly formidable. And at once she turned to one of the rose beds. 'Bessie Browns,' she said.

'I beg your pardon?'

'And Mildred Grants. I think they are my favourite Hybrid Teas.'

'Miss Minnychip, I do apologize. It's

simply that I've spent my entire working life jostling with crimes, and that I resent having my nose rubbed in another one in my old age.'

'But you have come to Clusters, have you not, quite of your own free will, because of what has happened to poor Oliver Osprey?'

'Yes, of course – and I do promise to be serious. I'll try to find out who killed him. I'll stick on the job until – until all those late roses droop and die, if need be.'

'Will it take that long?' There was now a hint almost of challenge in Miss Minny-chip's voice.

'I hope not. Perhaps a couple of days.' Appleby said this with some gravity, and it was with gravity that he looked at Miss Minnychip as he said it. 'And, now, may we go back to Osprey's collection – and conceivably to your father's collection, as well? I've gathered that what has happened here has made you more than a little apprehensive that something equally out of the way may occur in your own house. And that is reasonable enough. If the Osprey Collection of coins has been under threat, so may the neighbouring Minnychip Collection well be.'

'Exactly so, Sir John. It is why I feel that some police protection ought to be afforded to me in my own modest dwelling. But, now, please tell me. Have Lord Osprey's coins been successfully stolen, or have they not?'

'At this stage, Miss Minnychip, that question can't be answered. We simply don't know.'

'Don't know!'

'It certainly sounds absurd. But nobody seems to know just where Lord Osprey kept this very compendious treasure. Have you yourself ever seen it, by the way?'

'Definitely not. I used to hear a good deal about it in my father's time, of course. But I have never seen it, and have no idea where Oliver kept it. Marcus must know – Marcus Broadwater. He virtually looked after the things.'

'But he *doesn't* know. He has told me so, earlier this morning. When he and Lord Osprey had occasion to inspect the collection together, Lord Osprey simply wheeled it in. That is Mr Broadwater's expression.'

'Wheeled it in!'

'It sounds extremely absurd, I agree. Absurd but not inconceivable.'

'But if Oliver was killed in the library as a result of coming upon a thief there, it must surely be somewhere in the library that–'

'That the collection has its home? Not

necessarily. And here we come to that mysterious intruder. At dusk yesterday evening, when you yourself and several other people were in the library, Lord Osprey made to close the curtains over the big French window. It was apparently his habit to do so himself. But on this occasion he suddenly saw someone lurking just outside. He at once drew the curtains to, and told Bagot to investigate. Is that correct? I gather from Lord Osprey's son, Adrian, that you had just a glimpse of this lurking person yourself.'

'Yes. That was precisely what happened.'

'Would you be able to pick out the intruder in an identity parade?'

'Dear me, no, Sir John. It was all too momentary for that.'

'Was it a man, or a woman?'

'I suppose it was a man. But no doubt one would somehow suppose a lurking figure to be that of a man. I really don't know. It was, as I say, all over in a couple of seconds.'

'But now, Miss Minnychip, consider. It has been discovered that there is a perfectly practicable means of getting across the moat and up to the small and isolated terrace on the other side of the window. It becomes, so to speak, a vulnerable point in Clusters' defences. So Lord Osprey may have become uneasy about it a good deal later last night, come down here to reassure himself, and actually encountered an intruder. His murder may have been a direct consequence of that. But that the thief, or intending thief, made his entry by way of the library is only a weak indication that the collection was kept in – or indeed near – it. Supposing a thief to have informed himself in one way or another where the coins were actually kept (in which case it seems that he would have decidedly the advantage of the rest of us) he may have been encountered by Lord Osprey when he was already in possession of the collection – in which case he has it now. Or he may have been so encountered when beginning to make his way to it – in which case he may have been unnerved by his own bloody deed, and fled without seeking out his booty.'

'Surely, Sir John, it is improbable that the intending thief would make a merely preliminary foray across the moat and to that window simply to peer into a crowded room?'

'It's a good point.' Appleby was coming to have a considerable respect for Miss Minnychip's intelligence. Ringwood, indeed, would have spotted this difficulty at once.

But Ringwood, after all, was a professional. 'I suppose it conceivable,' Appleby went on, 'that the lurker's first intention was to make his way into the library while everybody was at dinner, and to stay doggo just outside until then.' Appleby thought for a moment. 'By the way,' he then said, 'just where do you keep what I'm sure must be called the Minnychip Collection in your own house? Or would you rather not divulge that even to a respectable retired policeman?'

'Sir John, you persist in making fun of me. It is, I suppose, a spinster's destiny. But at least I remain alert to sign or sound of it. The hearing ear, and the seeing eye, the Lord hath made even both of them. I try to use them as I may.'

'Now it is you who are making fun of me, Miss Minnychip. But mayn't I have an answer? It's a question, after all, that Ringwood is bound to put to you, if you insist on his providing you with a guardian bobby or two.'

'If you must know,' Miss Minnychip said, 'I keep my father's coins under my bed.'

'An excellent place.' Appleby appeared struck by something. 'I wonder,' he said, 'whether Lord Osprey too did precisely that?'

8

Having returned indoors with Miss Minny-chip, and thanked her for her assistance, Appleby was making his way back to the Music Saloon when he became aware of the measured approach of Bagot, the late Lord Osprey's butler. Bagot had the appearance of one who would regard all haste as unseemly, so that Appleby wondered what sort of speed he had contrived to make when sent to investigate the mystery of that mysterious intruder on the previous evening. And now Bagot halted before him.

'Sir John,' he then asked with some solemnity, 'would it be convenient to have a word with you?'

'Of course. Fire away.'

If Bagot's eyebrows failed faintly to elevate themselves before this brusquerie it was evident that some effort had been required to ensure that they stayed put.

'First then, I am instructed by her lady-ship to ask you whether Mr Ringwood will take luncheon.'

'I suppose so, Mr Bagot. Most people have something at that time of day.'

'You do not quite understand me, sir.'

'Of course I do. But Lady Osprey can't be very clear about my relationship with Mr Ringwood. It is not for me to advise her on whether or not to ask the Detective-Inspector to lunch. I can, however, tell you at once what his answer will be should you be sent to him direct. He is at Clusters in an official capacity which precludes him from anything of the kind. You yourself must understand that.'

'The thought has certainly been in my mind, Sir John.'

'Then that's that. But would it be stretching a point too far to propose that you and I have a further short talk?'

'Most willingly, Sir John. May I suggest that we step into my pantry? It affords all proper privacy. His late lordship occasionally dropped in on me there for a brief chat. But nobody else comes near it. Not, so far, even the Detective-Inspector.'

'Capital. That will suit most admirably.'

So they made their way to Bagot's secluded citadel. It contained a small desk, an enormous safe, a sink, and a couple of chairs. On a shelf near a low radiator, uncorked, stood several bottles of burgundy. Appleby recalled that all good butlers believe that burgundy must breathe.

'Do sit down,' Bagot said briskly.

So Appleby sat down. Bagot, who remained standing, surveyed his domain with satisfaction.

'Nowadays,' he said, 'I have to leave the silver to the women. But I continue, of course, to look after the decanters, and most of the better crystal. Will you take a glass of Madeira?'

'Most willingly,' Appleby said.

Bagot poured a glass of Madeira, but without venturing to pour another for himself. He did, however, sit down.

'There will be speculation,' he said. 'And gossip. And – I fear – scandal.'

'I don't know about scandal. But speculation and gossip are sure starters in an affair like this. Have you any theory about it all, Mr Bagot?'

'Not a theory, Sir John. It would be somewhat presumptuous to have exactly that. An idea or two: no more.'

'That's much my own present position, Mr Bagot. But I'd like to hear what your ideas are about this murder.'

'Are you not at once taking something for

granted, Sir John? It's my principal idea that there was no murder.'

'You interest me very much. Do you feel, perhaps, that Lord Osprey committed a suicide?'

'Not that either.'

'Dear me!' Appleby was momentarily nonplussed by this. 'I'm not at all clear what is left.'

'Accident. Pure accident. And no discredit reflected on anyone. Which is extremely important, is it not?'

'The truth's what is extremely important. We mustn't think to scramble away from it. But go on.'

'It appears that when his lordship's body was discovered by a housemaid early this morning, it was clad in pyjamas and a dressing-gown. He had gone to bed, one must suppose, but had continued to be worried about the intruder earlier in the evening. Lord Osprey was a nervous man– Very nervous, indeed.'

'I'd hardly have suspected it.' Appleby looked curiously at Bagot. 'But continue.'

'He may have gone to sleep, and come awake, believing he had heard some disturbance in the house. But he was also, you must understand, a man of considerable courage.

He at once made his way to the library, the focus of the earlier alarm. He may have believed that somebody was attempting to break in through the French window. So he armed himself.'

'Armed himself! However could he do that?'

'With some sort of dagger, Sir John, from those abundant trophies on the wall.'

'You have a point there, Mr Bagot.'

'Have you noticed the floor, Sir John?'

'Yes, I have. Noticing things is a habit of mine.'

'Parquetry, Sir John. And with a number of doubtless very valuable oriental rugs. The footing is treacherous, sir.'

'Is it, indeed? People have been known to tumble about on it?'

'His lordship, at least, must have tumbled. And to tragic effect, Sir John. His slip, unhappily, was fatal to him.'

'But, Mr Bagot, if all this were true, surely the weapon would have been found beside the body?'

'It would have occurred to his lordship that as things stood – or rather, lay – there must have been a danger of his being thought to have committed suicide. And that, in an English nobleman, would be widely regarded as disgraceful.'

'It's disgraceful to make away with one-self?'

'In the circle in which his lordship moved, decidedly so. So he managed to stagger to the wall and replace the weapon.'

'So that it would be supposed he had been murdered – and there's nothing disgraceful about that?'

'Precisely so, Sir John.'

'But, Mr Bagot, if – following this line of yours – somebody had the misfortune to be charged with the murder, and convicted, would there be anything unfortunate and disgraceful about that?'

'The question is hypothetical, Sir John. But I think a coroner's jury will bring in what is called an open verdict. Many of its members, after all, will be tenants or employees about the estate.'

It had by this time become clear to Appleby that Bagot was unlikely to be of much help on what might be called the speculative side of the Clusters affair. Decorum was the man's touchstone, and as neither murder nor suicide was a decorous activity for Lord Osprey to have been involved with, his death had to be accidental and the last seconds of his life positively edifying. But it would be injudicious to tell Bagot that he had been talking nonsense, since on the level of plain fact he might have something valuable to impart.

'I believe,' Appleby said, 'that a blood-stained weapon may be discovered very much as you suppose, and I have little doubt that Detective-Inspector Ringwood is having the point investigated at this moment. I shall, of course, tell him about your ideas. All communications in this matter are valuable and will be carefully considered. But may I pass on to a few quite routine questions?'

'Certainly, Sir John. I am at your disposal.'

'How many people dined here last night?'

'Ten.'

'Lord and Lady Osprey, Mr Adrian Osprey, Miss Minnychip, Mr Broadwater, and a Mr Quickfall. That's six. Who else?'

'Mr and Mrs Purvis. They are from London. I believe that Mr Purvis had business connections with his lordship.'

'Eight. And the other two?'

'Lady Wimpole and Miss Honoria Wimpole. I understand that Admiral Wimpole is at sea.'

'We must hope we don't remain there long ourselves. The party gathered, I understand, in the library before dinner?'

'They did, Sir John.'

'That's the custom with you here?'

'Except when there is a larger weekend house-party, when the drawing-room is used before dinner as well as after it. On this occasion, of course, the house-party was exceptionally small.'

'Small enough for you to be quite certainly aware whether everybody was present?'

'Most decidedly, Sir John.'

'They were all in the library as you were taking round sherry, and when this intruder made his momentary appearance?'

'Most assuredly they were.'

'So far, so good.' Appleby considered for a little. When not lured into speculation, Bagot, he was coming to feel, was a clear-headed and presumably reliable witness. 'And now,' he went on, 'I come to something else – and it's something I don't quite get the hang of. Lord Osprey sees this figure outside the French window, and he then rapidly closes the curtains and tells you to go and investigate. The most effective way for you to have done that, I'd have thought, was to have drawn back the curtains again, opened the French window, and stepped out to that little terrace or platform or whatever it's to be called, and looked about you. Instead of which, you simply left the room.'

'Certainly, Sir John. Not having been given any precise instructions by his lord-ship, I used my own discretion.'

'Would it have been the kind of discretion, Mr Bagot, that is known as the better part of valour?'

'There may have been a certain element of that.' Bagot was by no means discomposed. 'I recalled that the chauffeur, Robinson, was in the servants' hall. I summoned him, and we went out of the front door together. The principal causeway to Clusters was thus directly in front of us, and to our right the moat came right up to the house, until interrupted by the small terrace in question. We thus had a very clear view of the only spot on which any intruder might still be lurking. Nobody was visible.'

'The terrace, or platform, itself strikes me as rather an oddity. Has it always been there?'

'It, and the French window giving on it, are comparatively recent in date. At about the turn of the century, I believe it was. His lordship's grandfather, who was something of an eccentric with a taste for reading, took it into his head that it would be pleasant to step straight out of the library, and sit *en plein air* – surveying, no doubt, the beauties of nature. An eccentric person, as I have said. But in quite a refined way.'

'Having been thus supported by the useful Robinson, you returned to the library, and told Lord Osprey that nothing of an irregular kind was to be seen?'

'Just so, Sir John.'

'And then they all went in to dinner?'

'Just so.'

'The whole lot are here still?'

'They have all concurred in a suggestion from Mr Quickfall that they should remain, as planned, at least until this afternoon – collecting their thoughts, as it were, and making any statement that Mr Ringwood thinks it expedient to require from them. Yes, everybody is still at Clusters.'

'Except Mr Broadwater, who has gone off fishing.'

'Precisely so, Sir John. Mr Broadwater is very much a devotee of the rod.'

'That is something I am aware of.' Appleby thought briefly. 'To go back for a moment,' he then said. 'You are quite certain that neither you yourself, nor the chauffeur, was aware of any disturbance whatever, either in or over the moat?'

'There was nothing at all. Except, of course, the bats.'

'The bats!' Appleby was started. 'What bats?'

'They come, I believe, from a deserted barn at the home farm. And also, perhaps, from a neglected little boat-house on the farther side of the moat. Frequently at dusk they are darting here and there. I don't, myself, much care for the bats.'

'Like the children in Mr Brackley's choir.'

'I beg your pardon, sir?'

'No matter, Mr Bagot. And now I must join Mr Ringwood. I am most grateful for your help.'

9

Ringwood, Appleby supposed would be in the Music Saloon, drawing what support he could from his assistants on their platform. But on his way – and at Clusters the route from any *A* to any *B* always seemed lengthy – Appleby was pounced on (for the effect was of just that) by a small elderly man of prosperous but otherwise nondescript appearance.

'Sir John Appleby?' this person said.

'Yes.'

'My name is Purvis. You won't have heard of me.'

'Well, Mr Purvis, not, so to speak, at large. But as a weekend guest here, accompanied by Mrs Purvis, you have been mentioned to me by the butler.'

'Bagot. Yes, of course. You have been speaking to him because you are investigating this shocking affair?'

'I suppose I must be said to be doing that. But unofficially, as it were, and at the instance of Lady Osprey, who is good enough to think of me as a family friend. As for Bagot, he came at me rather as you are doing now, Mr Purvis. I have just left him, as a matter of fact. A communicative man. I wonder whether that description fits you too.'

Mr Purvis, as was not surprising, seemed a little startled by this. But he replied at once.

'I'd certainly like, Sir John, to communicate anything I have to communicate, relevant to this monstrous business. Did Bagot happen to mention me to you?'

'Only very briefly. He said you had business connections with the dead man.'

'True enough – although it might be a shade misleading. I am by profession an accountant. Purvis, Purvis and Purvis, Sir John.'

'How do you do?' It seemed to Appleby that, as an informal introduction had thus been performed, this reply was adequate for the moment.

'Come into this little room.' Mr Purvis made a gesture at a door behind him. 'If any room can be called little in this overgrown warren of a building. I believe it's called a writing-room. And as nobody ever writes anything worth speaking of at Clusters, it's sure to be empty.'

So they went into the writing-room. It certainly contained an enormous desk, equipped with every conceivable aid to correspondence.

'A mass of brass and glass.' Mr Purvis made his principal vowels as flat as could be. 'As Lord Curzon said when they took him into his room at the Foreign Office. Looking at the desk, you know, he said just that. "Take away that mass of brass and glass." Ha ha.'

Appleby, although not much impressed by this decidedly 'in' note, smiled politely, and sat down.

'You were, in fact, Lord Osprey's accountant?' he asked.

'Precisely not. Osprey employed some quite different firm. But he did have a chat with me about his affairs now and then. Making a joke of it, he said it came less expensive.'

'I see. Was he hard-up?'

'It rather depends on what you mean, Sir John. People of this sort' – and Mr Purvis contrived a gesture designed to take in the whole of Clusters – 'can't very well be hard-up in the sense of being uncertain about tomorrow's dinner. Not that you and I mayn't live to see that sort of situation. But, beyond that, it's anybody's guess, I'd say. And I've known Osprey to be quietly fishing around, more than once.'

'I'd rather suppose it to be his brother-in-law who goes in for that.'

Mr Purvis took a moment or two to get hold of this, and then laughed obligingly.

'Damned good!' he said. 'Poor old Marcus. Yes, indeed. But I mean that I've had Oliver asking me a thing or two that he might have hesitated to put to his regular accountant. Wondering, you know, on how he could put his hand on fifty thousand or so. To make things a bit easier all round. At least for a time. Yes. At least for a time.'

'Did it ever occur to you that he might flog that collection?'

'Collection, Sir John?'

'The coins. The Osprey Collection of ancient coins.'

'Oh, *that*. Does it really exist? I, for one, have never had a sight of it.'

'Lord Osprey certainly appears to have kept it tucked away. But he and Marcus Broadwater seem to have mulled over it together. Moreover – but it must have been a good long time ago – he and Miss Minny-chip's father were by way of confabulating as fellow-collectors. Or so the lady tells me.'

'I'll believe in it when I see it, Sir John. When I have sight of it. Yes.'

'Well, just grant it provisional existence for a moment, Mr Purvis. And suppose it to be a major hoard of the stuff. It could be parted with piecemeal and unobtrusively over a comparatively short period of time, wouldn't you say? And the total might come well into the hundreds of thousands bracket, I'd suppose. Not that I know much about such things.'

'True enough, Sir John. Decidedly true enough. And, viewed in that light, it might be a considerable temptation to a thief.'

'Exactly so, Mr Purvis. And it may explain why not many people know where he kept his doubloons or pistoles or whatever. Broadwater tells me *he* didn't. He tells me that when the two of them had occasion to mull over the collection together, Lord Osprey simply wheeled it in on a glorified trolley.'

'In which case Oliver wasn't trusting his own brother-in-law? I'll give it to you that he wasn't a very trusting person.'

'Have you ever been aware of him – on previous occasions, I mean – as apprehensive about burglars, or thieves of any sort? He certainly seems to have been quickly alarmed by the intruder at the window last night.'

'Nothing of the sort is within my recollection, Sir John. And I don't know that you and I appear to have been getting anywhere.'

'Patience,' Appleby said. 'Patience, and shuffle the cards.'

Ringwood was not in the Music Saloon. Appleby ran him to earth – a rather broad strip of earth – on the causeway leading up to the main portal of Clusters. He was staring moodily along the line of the moat. But as Appleby came up he turned and transferred his gaze to the massive building itself.

'What might be called rather a daunting pile – wouldn't you say, Sir John?'

'Certainly a very considerable woodpile in which to be hunting for a nigger, Mr Ringwood. But – do you know? – I notched up one of my earliest small successes in rather the same sort of place. Or, rather, the same *size* of place. It belonged not to a baron but a duke.'

'Scamnum Court. I read about it in the papers as a kid, sir, and I'm not sure it wasn't what first prompted me to become a copper.'

'Do you regret that?'

'I think, now, that I'd rather have run away to sea. That was my earlier idea. It would have been better fun.'

'Yes, indeed. Better the Atlantic or Pacific to gaze out over than this muddy ditch.' For a moment Appleby and Ringwood looked at one another comprehendingly, as disillusioned public servants are apt to do. 'But *à propos* of that,' Appleby went on, 'what about the little boatshed. Did they find it?'

'Certainly they did. It's round a corner, and just out of sight of us here. Full of snoozing bats. But there's a little dinghy, all right, together with a pair of sculls. And they've all been in the water no time ago.'

'The plot thickens, Ringwood. Or dampens, perhaps one should say. Would you conclude that our last night's intruder knew his way around?'

'It would certainly seem so.'

'You've got a man staying put there now? Shed and dinghy and sculls must all be examined minutely, wouldn't you say?'

'Of course, Sir John. There's an officer on guard until relieved.'

'Good. But the key to the mystery lies essentially in that confounded library. How minutely that has to be searched, I'm sure you know.'

'Certainly I do.' For a moment Ringwood permitted himself to sound faintly reproachful. 'They're working on it at this moment.'

'Every book, Ringwood.'

'And dusted for finger-prints, Sir John?' A tinge of irony accompanied this question.

'I wouldn't quite say that. But it's true, of course, of every weapon, likely or unlikely, in those damned trophies. Is there any sort of lavatory close to the library?'

'There's a little place of the sort just next door. Provided, I suppose, for anybody who'd been after a particularly dusty book.'

'H and C?'

'H and C?' Ringwood had to repeat this phrase before he understood it. 'I don't know. I haven't been told.'

'Perhaps you ought to have been. A murderer, you know, frequently seeks immediately to cleanse his weapon of blood. If he does so under cold water, he probably succeeds. But if hot water is available, and he uses that, the result is likely to be less satisfactory. Odd, but it's so.'

'I'll remember the point.' Ringwood managed to look suitably edified. 'What about yourself, sir? Have you made any progress?'

'I'm not at all confident that I have, although I've talked to several people. Two of them may be said to have accosted me. Bagot was the first of them. Apparently for the sake of spreading a decent decorum over his employer's end, he had concocted a theory of accidental death. Complete nonsense, and rather surprising from a reasonably intelligent man. And he didn't conceal the fact that he behaved with rather more caution than courage when Lord Osprey told him to go after the intruder last night. He ought to have gone straight out through the French window, don't you think? Instead of which, he hunted out the chauffeur, and together they viewed the scene from a respectful distance. And that reminds me. What do we know about the latch or catch or bolt on that window?'

'I've looked into it, Sir John. There are two bolts, and normally they are kept pushed home so as to secure the window. But they are quite surprisingly flimsy affairs, and it rather looks as if a good shove had recently been given from outside and they'd tumbled out of place, so that one wing of the window might have been swung open.' Ringwood paused for a moment on this. 'It's rather a crucial point, I'd say.'

'It may certainly be that. In fact, it affects our investigation a good deal.'

'Undoubtedly, Sir John.'

'It at least bears an appearance of fitting in with a general picture of the affair.' Appleby, who possessed the trick of getting much caution into a few words, was silent for a moment. 'The other fellow who came at me,' he then said, 'was the guest called Purvis. He's an accountant by trade, but he doesn't act professionally or officially for the Ospreys. He contrived to hint that Lord Osprey may have been hard-up after a fashion. I rather felt, Ringwood, that the fellow only wanted to stare at me. And I'm blessed if he didn't then tell me that our talk seemed to be getting nowhere.'

'What about you and me, Sir John? Are we getting anywhere?'

'I don't know that we are. What would you say to taking a little time off? A rather more abundant breath of fresh air than we get just standing here and mooning? Exercise, Ringwood! We'll find that boat-house and take out the dinghy. That's what we'll do. Come along.'

10

If Detective-Inspector Ringwood found this sudden aquatic enthusiasm on Sir John Appleby's part bewildering and even a shade unbecoming, he managed to keep the fact to himself – with the result that the two men found themselves within a few minutes entering the little moat-side shed which had hitherto existed, so to speak, only on the outer margin of the story. It was dilapidated but not damp, shadowy but not dark, and it was true that numerous bats were depending in a comfortable snooze from its small rafters. Rather less comfortable was a constable sitting on an upturned bucket.

'It's been in the water, all right,' Appleby said, looking at the dinghy. 'You and I and the officer had better agree on the fact here and now – just in case, on some future occasion, a barrister has to elicit more evidence on the point than is provided by the man or men you've already sent here. You agree?'

'The boat has certainly been afloat quite recently. And you can even feel some moisture still on the sculls.' Ringwood spoke with the relief of a man suddenly discovering in a companion something other than insanity or simple whimsy. 'And we push it out and embark, do we?'

'Just that. There's even a little rudder. I'll take that and you take the sculls – and it's hard to starboard for a start until we have sight of that little terrace and the French window. And you can see from here that the so-called moat just isn't, nor ever has been, a moat in the simple sense of the term. Clusters, as everybody knows, is simply planted on an island in the middle of a big pool.'

'And a muddy sort of pool at that. In places it's all silted up. If you or I, Sir John, lived surrounded by such a thing, we'd have the sanitary people after us in no time.'

'I don't doubt it.' By this time the dinghy was on the water and moving. 'But – dash it all! – it's suddenly quite deep, isn't it? The bottom must be a matter of mini-ravines and mini-mountains. How very odd! Heave ho, Ringwood, heave ho!'

This wholly inapposite nautical injunction was perhaps to be forgiven Sir John Appleby since – and for the first time that day – he was in a state of considerable excitement.

'There's the terrace,' he said, 'and there's the window. We'll make straight for them now.' As he spoke, he gave a pull on the rudder – and, almost at once, the dinghy came to a stop, with its bow up and its stern almost in the water. 'Back paddle, Ringwood,' he said. 'We've run into one of the mini-mountains.'

Ringwood did as he was told, to an effect of immediate disengagement. He peered over the side.

'Your mountain can be nothing but a mud bank, sir,' he said. 'And we've stirred up quite a dollop of it.'

'So we have. But row ahead. We'll try a bit further on.'

Ringwood complied, but almost immediately it was with the same result.

'It's like a submerged maze,' he said irritably. 'And there are people watching us from the windows. I can see some of my own men. They must think us crazy.'

'Which is very much what we are not, my dear fellow.' Appleby's excitement still showed in his speech. 'And to speak of a maze is a little to exaggerate, you know. There's nothing man-made involved, I'd say. But to paddle even this small craft around, you need an exact knowledge of the terrain –

not that terrain is exactly the word.'

'What you need, it seems to me, is to be a bloody submarine.' Ringwood was breathing heavily – and not entirely from the exertion of tugging at his oars. 'And don't imagine I've no notion of what we are about.'

'I'm never likely to imagine anything of the sort.' Appleby was enjoying this loosening up of his relations with the Detective-Inspector. 'So just what have we proved, so far?'

'That nobody can get into this little tub and simply row straight over to that French window.'

'Quite so. And what have we still to find out?'

'Whether it can be done at all – fairly rapidly if one's familiar with the lie of the land.'

'Or of the moat. Quite so. Could an oarsman who is familiar with what we may call the maze manage it – or would he know he couldn't? It must be possible for this dinghy to potter fairly freely here and there on the moat. There'd be no point in its being here at all if that weren't so. But just round about that little terrace and French window there may be what might be called a no-go area. Swimming, or at least wading through

115

patches of fairly deep water, would be required. Of course we don't know whether or not that intruder was dripping wet. Or muddy up to, say, the waist.'

'Mud to that extent, Sir John, would probably show up on the terrace, where there's no sign of anything of the kind. And if the fellow performed his manoeuvre a second time, and then actually broke into the library and killed Lord Osprey, his leaving plenty of mud around would be a dead certainty.'

'Absolutely true. So we must go on searching – rather like the fellows who went seeking the North-West Passage. Frobisher and that crowd, I mean.'

Ringwood, already tugging again at his oars, offered no pretence of being amused by this comparison.

'We'll go up to the causeway,' he said. 'No getting beyond that, of course, although there may be a conduit or two running through it. But if we want mud, there we have it. Silted up against the stonework, and several feet deep. We turn just short of that, keep on nosing towards the house, may or may not be baffled any number of times, and may or may not find there is a way through.'

'Just that,' Appleby said.

And there was. In the end, and after many false casts, Appleby had only to put out a hand and steady the dinghy against the terrace.

'Odd,' he said, 'that they never thought to have at least a low balustrade. But here we are, and I suppose we can get back again. But what if anything, Ringwood, does our trip tell us?'

'That somebody got into this dinghy last night, and then – whether just once or again later – made his way here and back.'

'And rapidly, Ringwood. Without anything like our sort of trial and error. Knowing the route well.'

'How do you make that out, Sir John?'

'Bagot mayn't have been in a great hurry to collect that chauffeur and make his way along the causeway to a commanding view of this whole area. He was probably scared, and as dilatory as he could reasonably be. But if the two men saw nothing out of the way, the intruder making off again in this dinghy must have regained the boat-house pretty quickly. So who can he have been? Or, to put the question more cautiously, to what category of persons can he – or she, for that matter – have belonged?'

'Surely, Sir John, it could hardly have been a female? The whole pictures suggests what may be called a masculine crime.'

'I rather agree. But the only testimony on the point is Miss Minnychip's. And she has spoken to me – and I suppose to you – of no more than a mere impression that it was a man. And an impression gained in the dusk and from a mere glimpse. But let us assume, at least for the moment, that it was a man who rowed over here and approached the French window. Have we, so far, the slightest clue to his identity? Or, failing that, what may be called a mere instinctive suspicion?'

'What about that fellow who has insisted on clearing off and going fishing? Lady Osprey's brother, Marcus Broadwater?'

'Absolutely out, Ringwood. And as one of a whole category of persons. Everyone, you may say, on view so far! Bagot asserts that the whole family, together with the little clump of weekend guests, were in the library drinking his sherry when the thing happened. Bagot, of course may be mistaken. Or he may be lying outright. But check up on the point, and it's my guess the whole lot will subscribe to the fact.'

'They do, Sir John. I've made sure of it.'

The Detective-Inspector said this almost as if he were ashamed of his own promptitude and thoroughness. 'So suggesting Broadwater is mere muddle.'

'It's the impulse we all have, in our line of business, to see any affair of this sort as what may be called a closed-shop case. We have to face it. But the person operating from this wretched cockle-shell is, so to speak, out there in the void. At least in this part of the inquiry, Ringwood, we're after a Great Unknown.' Appleby paused on this melodramatic exclamation. 'Of course it might be the vicar,' he said.

'The vicar, Sir John?' Reasonably enough, Ringwood was merely bewildered by this.

'Mr Brackley. He may have got rather seriously at odds with Lord Osprey over the bats.'

'I think, Sir John' – and Ringwood managed to produce a dutiful smile – 'we'd better, perhaps, paddle back to the shed.'

11

Having returned to *terra firma* after this odd watery excursion, the two men walked in silence along the causeway to the house. Ringwood then went back to the Music Saloon. Appleby lingered in the main Entrance Hall. This, being in what has to be called the modern part of Clusters, was a large and lofty oval sheathed in white marble from top to bottom and paved in white marble too. You could have put a dozen fairground giants in it and it would still have had a dispeopled look – the impression of emptiness arising partly from a circumference rich in out-size and vacant marble niches which seemed to be waiting to house answeringly colossal statues which had failed to arrive from Greece or Italy. Perhaps, Appleby thought, they had been lost in the post. Traversing this expanse – and for the moment thus fancifully disposed – he told himself he knew what it must be like to be a small spider making its way along the bottom of a bath.

But now a second spider (so to speak) appeared in the form of an elderly man, silvery-haired and slightly stooped, but over six feet tall all the same. And this superior spider came to a halt before him and spoke with grave courtesy.

'Sir John Appleby?' the superior spider said.

'Yes, I am Appleby.'

'My name is Rupert Quickfall, Sir John. I am a barrister, and a friend – or, perhaps better, an acquaintance – of the late Lord Osprey. I have never been to Clusters before, and now it is fairly certain that I shall never be here again. You may have heard of me as the man who has insisted that, at least for the time, poor Osprey's household and guests should all stay put.'

'And quite rightly,' Appleby said. 'This sensible man, Detective-Inspector Ringwood, can get statements from everybody straight away.'

'And you yourself can at least take a look at us.'

'I am glad, Mr Quickfall, that you express it just so. There is no question of my having been, as it were, called out of retirement to poke around. I happen to live not far away, and have come over to afford Lady Osprey what support I can.' Appleby produced this piece of humbug (as it had now undeniably become) quite unblushingly.

'How very good of you! We understand one another perfectly, do we not? There is equally no question of my becoming professionally involved, although it so happens that I work at the criminal bar. Ah, retirement! It is a magical word with me. But I can't afford it: positively not. I have to devil away. I couldn't afford even to accept the leisure of the bench, should so unlikely a notion as promoting me to it enter the Lord Chancellor's head. And coping with endless stupid crimes! It hasn't even the intellectual appeal that eases the lot of my colleagues in chancery. But, as I was saying, here at Clusters you and I are simply knowledgeable lookers-on, like fellows who have once batted for England but now merely sit in the pavilion, sucking their pipes.'

'Some of them, of course, have to watch the form closely, in order to pick the right men for the next test match. But, Mr Quickfall, I don't know that the sporting analogy is at all an appropriate one. Here is murder.'

'I couldn't agree more.' Quickfall made an elegant and no doubt practised forensic gesture. 'But there is likely to be – we must certainly hope there will be – a criminal trial arising out of this abominable affair. I might even be called upon to examine you in the witness-box.'

'I think not, Mr Quickfall. Having been in at the death, so to speak, you surely couldn't with any propriety accept a brief in the matter.'

'But of course not! How right you are. But we can, at least, discuss the affair informally, here and now. Each of us is an expert after his fashion, is he not?'

'Certainly we can exchange information. And I've told you how I come to be at Clusters. What about yourself? You say you have never been here before, and are un-likely to be here again. So you don't con-sider yourself to be a friend of the Osprey family. What has brought you here on this sole occasion?'

'What I was trying to convey, Sir John, was that I am in no sense a *family* friend of the Ospreys. But poor Osprey himself I have known for many years. Or, rather, I knew for many years.' Quickfall paused fractionally on this, and Appleby reflected that here was a man well accustomed to thinking rapidly on his feet. 'One's tenses are apt to go wrong, are they not,' Quickfall then continued, 'when something so sudden as this has happened? But it is my point that I did know the dead man himself over a long period of years. We were at school together near Windsor' – and again Quickfall made a momentary pause, as if to let the magnificence of this modest periphrasis sink in – 'and belonged to the same club. Indeed, we lunched together there not infrequently. So my coming down to Clusters on what must be called a rather delicate and confidential occasion was entirely in order. But I will not, of course, let that confidentiality interfere with what I tell you, my dear Appleby.' This swift move from 'Sir John' belonged to the same order of rhetoric as had the avoidance of 'Eton'. 'I came down to size up – and give what advice I could on – what was distinctly a family crisis. The trouble, as I understood it, concerned the Lord Osprey who now is.'

'Adrian?'

'I had little doubt about that, although Lord Osprey rather tended to confusion and self-contradiction. The fact that he was talking to me over a telephone line seemed to make him uneasy. But I concluded that Adrian had got mixed up with a young woman in what may be termed a different sphere of society. There had, it seems, been a suggestion – and a suggestion accompanied by threats and demands – that the young woman had been obstinately uncompliant. I was at least able to gather that as being the nub of the matter.'

'Do you mean that Adrian Osprey raped the girl?' Appleby uttered this sharply. The question was among the nastier of the many uncomfortable questions he had been obliged to ask in the course of his career.

'Precisely so. And I have been hoping to establish that the allegation is stuff and nonsense.'

'Is the girl known to be habitually lax in sexual behaviour?'

'It's a point undetermined so far. But, if it be so, there would in no sense be an absolute end to the matter. In law, as you no doubt know, a proven drab may suffer rape as definitely as a duchess.'

'No doubt. And there is clear evidence that Adrian was, as you put it, a little rough with this uncompliant partner?'

'Her father apparently took her straight to a doctor, who is asserted to have found a good deal of bruising on her. Osprey's main point was that the father might be coped with.'

'*Coped with,* Quickfall?'

'He felt that the man judged there was money in it.'

So here was something much more clear-cut than indeterminate skulduggeries in the field of numismatics. And what it required, for a start, was an appraisal of human character. Appleby's first impression had been of a violent young man, of a door flung open and a constable showing some evidence of having been shoved or thumped vigorously aside. Adrian Osprey had then advanced upon Appleby with an uncivil injunction to clear out. He had subsequently offered some less disobliging remarks, but immediately followed them with the assertion that policemen in general have a nasty smell. After that, he had settled down to supplying a fair amount of useful information on the sensational event of the previous evening – but always with a hint of violence in his choice of phrase. As an exhibition of character, it all added up to very little. It was quite possible, indeed, to imagine the new Lord Osprey being 'a little rough' (as Quickfall had cautiously expressed it) with a village girl. Such girls often led such young men on in that way, and then got frightened

– at which point the young men got frightened too, reflected that beyond a certain point that sort of thing simply wasn't on, and disisted with apologies and awkward laughter. The Adrian Osprey of Appleby's slender acquaintance fitted into that sort of picture easily enough. Beyond that, it was at present impossible to go.

'What about the father of this girl?' Appleby asked. 'He turned up on Osprey Senior, did he, and demanded monetary compensation?'

'Dear me, no. Osprey rang me up at once, but I only got here yesterday morning. We hadn't yet discussed it when he was murdered.'

Perhaps unreasonably, Appleby felt this to be astonishing information.

'But at least,' he said, 'you've had some cautious conversation with Adrian about the thing?'

'By no means, Appleby. I had decided to begin some serious inquiry today. But last night's extraordinary events – first that affair at the window, and later Osprey's shocking death – have left me, I confess, something at a loss. Hence my seeking this discussion with you.'

'Have you told Detective-Inspector Ring-wood about this?'

'Not yet. But it is of course incumbent on me to do so. Having now talked it over with you, I'll seek him out at once.' Quickfall hesitated for a moment. 'It is an extremely serious matter, is it not?'

'Certainly it is.'

'And we shan't, my dear Appleby, hear any more about your being at Clusters merely to condole with Lady Osprey?'

For a moment Appleby felt this to be an impertinence, but then he decided it was fair enough.

'No,' he said. 'You will not.'

12

The gentle reader may have observed that, halfway through this narrative of untoward events at Clusters, several female characters have yet to make their bow. Mrs Purvis is one of them: the wife of that accountant from whom – such is the vanity of human wishes – the now deceased Lord Osprey had been hoping to receive a few useful tips on how to raise a more or less modest sum of ready money. But since Lord Osprey has been murdered – and unless Mr Purvis turns out to be the unlikely criminal – Mrs Purvis seems destined to remain more or less in the wings.

Miss Jane Minnychip, indeed, has appeared and has had a good deal to say: both about bats in the scheme of divine providence, and as herself the guardian of a collection of ancient coins brought together by her deceased father, Sir Philip Minnychip, an eminent Indian Civil Servant. Miss Minnychip, moreover, is on the record as having glimpsed the person described by Lord

Osprey through that problematical French window. It seems likely, therefore, that Miss Minnychip will again take the centre of the stage a little later on.

Another, and much younger, woman has just been heard of. She is a publican's daughter, and nameless so far. This latter fact is in itself suspicious – but suspicious, as it were, the wrong way on. She may well be taken, that is to say, as no more than a red herring, who will drop out unobtrusively in the sequel. But, of course, one never can tell.

Two other women have been mentioned, but still linger in the wings. They are Lady Wimpole (whose husband, the Admiral, is at sea) and her daughter, Honoria. And here they are. Both have made statements to Detective-Inspector Ringwood, and they are now in Lady Wimpole's bedroom, waiting to be called to luncheon, and meanwhile packing suitcases in a desultory way. They hope to leave Clusters in the course of the afternoon, but are resigned to spend another night in the place, if it is required of them.

What is immediately interesting in these ladies is their evident appearance of having little in common. Both, indeed, suggest membership of the same upper or middling order of society, but any similarity ends there. Viewed sitting side by side in a railway carriage, they would quite fail to hint any connection one with the other. Lady Wimpole (although in an unobtrusive way comfortable with her years) is very well groomed and turned out. Her attire, indeed, is so comprehensively correct for one who is spending a weekend in the country that you are at once aware of it as coming from an expensive establishment in London. Honoria, on the other hand, is dressed rather at random in what might be termed a functional and slightly mannish way, but this somehow makes more evident the fact of her being a strikingly good-looking young woman. Even horn-rimmed spectacles of a round and distinctly utilitarian sort fail to disguise this very important fact.

What mother and daughter do share is something by its nature not immediately apparent to the view. They are both women of strong character, and each sets considerable store on getting a good deal of her own way in the world. Their ambitions, however, differ widely.

Lady Wimpole is determined that her husband shall become First Sea Lord, and on the strategy and tactics requisite for this she manages to keep surprisingly up-to-date. When she was a girl, a sailor of her husband's present seniority would have been well poised for this ultimate promotion were he in command of the Mediterranean Fleet. It isn't quite like that now. The Mediterranean Fleet – some disagreeably plain-speaking persons are given to asserting – has fallen within a notional rather than an actual category. Certainly it hangs much in the dusty rear (to employ a markedly dissonant metaphor) of American Armadas in that region. Northern Approaches are another matter. Their importance is the reason for Lady Wimpole's seeing to it that Admiral Wimpole has to spend quite a lot of time not all that far away from the North Pole.

But nothing of all this accounts for the Wimpole ladies' presence at Clusters now. An obscure backwoods peer is not likely to have much influence at the Admiralty, or on the cabinet or a prime minister. But Lady Wimpole is ambitious for her daughter as well as for her husband. This is why she accepted poor Lady Osprey's weekend invitation when it came along. Why Honoria very readily agreed to accompany her will appear quite soon.

'And so unexpected!' Lady Wimpole said.

'Of course it was that, Mama.' Honoria Wimpole wedged rather a bulky book into a corner of her dressing-case. 'You almost speak as if you were surprised at the thing's surprisingness. Of course it was unexpected. Nobody expected Lord Osprey to be so disagreeably murdered – or, indeed, murdered at all. Unless, I suppose, the man who did the murder. And perhaps he didn't expect it, either. We haven't been told much, but it does sound as if it had been rather an impromptu affair.'

'One can't help reflecting that it changes Adrian's future dramatically. Now, can we, dear?'

'It certainly changes the young man's situation. About his future, one just doesn't know.'

'I fail to see any real distinction, Honoria. You are rather too fond of drawing distinctions, it seems to me. I put it down to Oxford and that absurd fellowship at your college there. Who ever heard of a woman being a fellow? Of course, I quite acknowledge that *that* was a distinction, and a credit to the family, and so on. Your father was extremely pleased. But there *are* other sides of life that have to be considered.'

'Birth, and copulation, and death.'

'My dear Honoria!' Lady Wimpole, unaware that this summation of things had been offered by an extremely high Anglican, was greatly shocked.

'And just what was absurd about that fellowship?'

'Of course nothing at all, dear. I spoke too hastily. Only, for a woman to be called a fellow does sound a little odd. When one talks about a jolly good fellow one means something the same as calling a man a nice chap.'

'What a very silly conversation.' Honoria, although a reasonably dutiful daughter, did occasionally find her mother getting on her nerves. 'Anyway, I'm not a fellow any more. I'm a curator. Of course, I could ask the Director if I might be called a curatrix, explaining that my mother would like it better.'

'Do come back to Adrian Osprey, dear, and talk sense. It's his changed prospects that are so unexpected. He might have had thirty years ahead of him – or even longer than that – simply as the heir to a title, perhaps on slender means. Not that *that* wouldn't be something.'

'I haven't heard of him as doing much to

enlarge his means. Has he any profession? I certainly don't recall its having been mentioned in the course of family chat.'

'It's a *difficult* position for a young man to be in, Honoria. And, of course, it's early days with dear Adrian yet. He is so *very* young.'

'Younger than I am by several years, I rather think.'

'And there's certainly a point *there*.' Lady Wimpole was so convinced of the cogency of this that her speech almost became impressive. 'There is a tide in the affairs of men,' she said unexpectedly, 'which, taken at the flood, leads on to fortune. But–'

'So, Mama, you pretty well want the funeral baked meats coldly to furnish forth the marriage tables. The death of Oliver Osprey in one column of *The Times*, and my engagement to Adrian Osprey in another column of the same issue.'

Lady Wimpole, who had given immediate thought to this point, and had decided that a week, or even ten days, should separate these announcements, was very justly offended by this last speech on her daughter's part.

'Really, Honoria,' she said, 'if you have only the most frivolous thoughts about Adrian – an honourable young man (nobleman, indeed) who is ready to be devoted to you–'

'Now we come to sheer nonsense.' Honoria suddenly gave signs of being really angry. 'What scrap of evidence have you got that Adrian is prepared to do anything of the sort? He seems to me to be rather a decent young man, if in a somewhat immature and *farouche* way, but I am very sure he hasn't been making eyes at me. If he did, if he were to ask me to marry him, I'd refuse him on the instant. And I'd tell him to go away and find a nice girl of his own age, with his own tastes and interests. Or, for that matter, with his own lack of anything of the kind.'

Had Lady Wimpole been a perceptive woman, she might have derived some comfort from the very extremity of this. As it was, she simply lost patience with Honoria.

'If *that's* what you feel,' she cried, 'I don't know what can have prompted you to accept Lady Osprey's invitation to Clusters.'

'I've come to Clusters with you simply because I judged the invitation to be extremely opportune.'

'So it was, my dear. *Most* opportune. With Adrian–'

'We are not thinking, Mama, of the same opportunity. It was Lord Osprey, and not his son, who was in my head. You see, I'd been corresponding with Lord Osprey, and

I wanted to establish a closer contact with him.'

'*Corresponding ... closer contact?*' It was clear that unspeakable images had momentarily presented themselves to Lady Wimpole's vision. But with an effort she controlled herself. 'Honoria,' she said, 'just what do you mean?'

'I mean for one thing, Mama, that you keep on ignoring my profession. Numismatics, Mama. Coins. It so happens that I curate them. Just as that brother of Lady Osprey's does. Marcus Something.'

'Broadwater, my dear.' Before her daughter's sudden vehemence, Lady Wimpole was confused and placatory. 'And *of course* you have your profession. One hears nowadays of so many girls having professions. And your father and I are both very pleased about it. Only, I am sorry you have to work in that dull old museum, and not at the Mint. The Mint is the *Royal* Mint, you know, so I am sure it must have the nicest coins. But what has this to do with Oliver Osprey?'

'I must have told you several times that he has – or had, since he's now dead – a rather notable collection of coins which he has always been very cagey about. I wanted to learn something about them, and in particular whether he really possessed two or three unique things he'd been known to brag about. But when I wrote to him he sent me only brief replies and blank refusals. Then I happened to run into him at a party in town, and I nobbled him and chatted him up. And finally he said that the next time we came to stay with him here at Clusters, he would show me this and that. It was all slightly absurd, because the Osprey Collection certainly isn't one of the great private collections, and yet his lordship seemed to make quite a privilege of the thing. It was rather as if the last female he'd shown the coins to had been Queen Mary. If it *had* been, I'll bet she'd have possessed herself of something pretty valuable to remind her of a delightful occasion. You know what she was.'

'Honoria, dear, I've had to tell you several times that it's bad form to make fun of the Royal Family. Your grandfather never made fun of Dickie, although it would have been fairly easy to do sometimes.'

'Who in the world was Dickie, Mama?'

'He was a great-grandson of Queen Victoria, Honoria. And he became, among other things, First Sea Lord, as his father had been before him.' Lady Wimpole was clearly displeased at her daughter's ignorance of these quasi-dynastic matters. 'But what about those coins you were so interested in? Did poor Oliver in fact show them to you?'

'No, indeed, Mama. No such luck. I think he meant to do so either today or tomorrow. But, instead, he got himself killed. It was vexatious of him, was it not? What I have to do now, of course, is to chat up Adrian. I suppose he inherits the things, along with everything else. Only – as I've made clear to you, Mama – he isn't going to inherit *me*.'

13

While this conversation was going on, Appleby had sought out Ringwood, and found him in the library. Two policemen, a sergeant and a constable, were hard at work taking the books in careful handfuls from the shelves, flashing a torch into the cavity thus exposed, and then putting the books back again. They clearly found this dull and sweaty work, but were uncomplaining, nevertheless. Ringwood, on the other hand, was excited and almost triumphant.

'Speed!' he said to Appleby. 'Impetus! It's the royal road to successful investigation. Think of that dreadful affair in Yorkshire, Sir John. Dozens of men bogged down in front of one or another card-index, and the horror going on all the time. Get off to a flying start, and it's likely to be different. And we've done it. At least, we've found the weapon. Or are pretty sure we have. Thanks to you, sir. The trophies, you know. We went to work on them at once – and, sure enough, there the thing was. The weapon, Sir John.'

'That sounds most promising, Ringwood. Tell me about it.'

'It was there, sir.' And Ringwood pointed to one of the elaborate trophies flanking the fire. 'You can see the vacant space. It was back in the position it came from, but the webbing holding it there was half cut through – as if it had been snatched out, or shoved back in a great hurry. That alerted us – was enough to alert us.' Ringwood paused, as if to receive due commendation for this highly efficient exercise. 'No blood on it, Sir John, or none visible to the naked eye. But I remembered about that wash-place, and what you said about hot and cold water. And, in there, we found what was certainly a minute spot of blood on a tile. We got up the tile, and I sent both off instantly to the forensic people. If they do detect blood on the blade, they'll ring through in about an hour's time.'

'Good work,' Appleby said briskly. 'What sort of a weapon was it?'

'I'd call it a dagger halfway to becoming a sword. Ugly affair, and with an Eastern look to it. More than that, I couldn't say, not having made a study of such things.'

'Perhaps an Osprey brought it back from some verge of our far-flung empire, Ringwood, about a hundred years ago. Have you tried to think just how it could have done its job? Somebody unknown used it to kill Lord Osprey – or so manipulated it that Lord Osprey died as a result. For us it comes to the same thing, but they wrangle over such points at a criminal trial. There's more to it than that, however. Just before dinner last night, there was the alarming business of the unknown intruder out there on the terrace. Suppose that, much later, Lord Osprey was somehow prompted to return, very much on his own, to this room. It must have been in a wary or apprehensive state of mind, wouldn't you say? When he did encounter somebody – as he certainly did, or he'd be alive today – he would be very much on his guard, would he not?'

'Certainly, Sir John. Unless, of course, the person he encountered had what you may call a reassuring identity.'

'Quite so. But now, Ringwood, imagine yourself to be that reassuring person. Then imagine some sort of more or less un-expected dispute or quarrel. Lord Osprey, so thoroughly scared earlier in the evening, would surely be speedily on the *qui vive* now. And you have to wrench this dagger from its place on the wall and cut his lordship's throat with it. From in front? From behind? Try to imagine yourself going to work, Ringwood.'

'It's not too easy an exercise, Sir John.' Although a serious man, the Detective-Inspector allowed himself a brief smile. 'But one thing's certain. The murder must have happened very quickly. There can't have been much of a face-to-face struggle, or not of a kind that would leave any signs on the corpse. And the killer must have known what was to hand, there on the wall. The library was familiar to him.'

'You may have a point there.' Appleby thought for a moment. 'I wonder whether Lord Osprey ever did business in this room – interviewed tenants: that sort of thing?'

'Inquiries can be made, sir. But, at a guess, I'd say not. There's a room they call his lordship's private office in another part of the building. And a quick-witted man, although a stranger to this library, might glance at the wall there, and tumble to the fact that there was an abundance of weapons pretty well within arm's reach.'

'Don't touch it, George, for the love of Mike!'

This urgent injunction, delivered at the far end of the library by the sergeant of police to the constable, had the effect of cutting short what was becoming a somewhat speculative conversation. And then the sergeant called out to his superior officer from across the room.

'Something odd here, sir. It's a key.'

The shelving in the library at Clusters was not of any newfangled adjustable sort. It marched all round the chamber in severe straight lines, regardless of whether it was supporting folios, quartos, octavos, or even duodecimos. And it was behind a row of uniformly diminutive books that the officers had made their discovery. It was certainly a key: neither very big nor very small; a middling sort of key such as might be found in any door. It was quite a plain key, but somehow intimated that it wasn't a plebeian key. It seemed, in fact, to belong to a time in which even utilitarian objects had to own a certain elegance if they were to aspire to use among the upper ranges of society.

'The dust,' Appleby said.

The area (and it was of considerable depth) behind that on which the small books had been ranged lay beneath a substantial film of dust: much more dust than a self-respecting librarian would have been at all inclined to tolerate. But Clusters had no librarian; had probably never had a librarian; was not a nobleman's country seat of quite that order of grandeur. No doubt the flat nozzle of a vacuum cleaner was run over the tops of the books in a perfunctory way by a bored housemaid, but beyond that the dust was undisturbed except by an occasional mouse.

'No dust on the key,' Ringwood said. 'It hasn't been hidden there long.'

'It *is*, in one sense, hidden,' Appleby said. 'But not in another. I mean that it hasn't been intentionally hidden there by anyone. Or I don't think it has.'

'Just how do you make that out, sir?' The Detective-Inspector was not one for concealing his perplexities and looking wise. 'It seems to me as if somebody has been standing just there, holding the key. And he hasn't wanted to acknowledge the fact. So, standing with his back to the shelving and his hands behind him, he has slipped the thing over the top of these little books, and let it drop.'

'But wouldn't that be an awkward manoeuvre to carry out, Ringwood? You might have a shot at it and see. And there's another point. The key doesn't seem to me to have *dropped*. It can only be said to have *skidded* – and for rather a long way on a diagonal line from just behind the books to almost the back of the shelf. If it were a boat, it might be spoken of as leaving a small wake behind it – only, instead of disturbed water, there's disturbed dust. It's a pretty minute effect, but perfectly perceptible. Don't you agree?'

'I think I do. But what's the inference, sir?'

'A sudden and alarming situation at the other end of the room, near the French window. Possibly this end is in something like darkness. Darkness may suggest security to a man in a panic. Osprey has the key, but doesn't want it discovered. He panics, and hurls it away from him into that saving darkness. By sheer chance it skims across the top of these little books on a diagonal line, and comes to rest where your men have now spotted it. What do you think?'

'It sounds a bit far-fetched to me, Sir John.'

'So it is.' Appleby approved at once of this forthright speech on Ringwood's part. 'But let's think about the key itself. Whether dropped or chucked, it remains a definite problem. Where does it fit?'

'Where, indeed.' Ringwood permitted himself a chuckle at the ambiguity of this question. 'At a guess, it's the key to a room or cupboard in this unnatural warren of a place.'

'It's a good guess – but, still, a guess. We must test it out. Try it. In every lock.'

'Good God, Sir John!' The Detective-Inspector was aghast. 'It would take one can't say how many hours to do anything of the sort. It's not as if one could set a dozen men on the job. Or not unless one could have a locksmith cut as many replicas.'

'Quite so. And, of course, the key may be to something not here at Clusters, at all. But I doubt that. I think it probably fits a lock here on the ground floor of Clusters.'

'The ground floor, sir? How do you make that out?'

'Another guess, I'm afraid. I'm supposing that the key gives access to that collection.'

'Collection, Sir John?'

'The Osprey Collection of coins, Ringwood. We know that Lord Osprey was idiosyncratically cagey on the numismatic front. And we know that he produced his hoard for his brother-in-law, Marcus Broadwater, on a trolley. Broadwater, you know, is a professional numismatist, who advised him – cataloguing the things, and so forth.'

'He must have been off his rocker – Lord Osprey must. A trolley, you say!'

'Quite so. But the point is that, since Clusters doesn't seem to run to any lifts or hoists, the coins were kept in concealment here on the ground floor. And it's possible that this key may lead to them.'

'So you think, sir, that the collection of

coins is near the heart of the matter?'

'It's no more than a conjecture at this stage, Ringwood. I've come across one or two elements that don't seem to fit into any such notion. But here is this mysterious key, which *does* fit. And it must, literally, fit some lock or other. We've got to find it.'

'The point is one you need scarcely reiterate, Sir John.' It was clear that these two policemen – active and retired – were not getting on very well together. 'The sergeant here can begin going round with the key at once. Only we'd better have a photograph of the thing here on the shelf before disturbing it. And let the finger-print people see it's quite without a surface they could work on.'

'Quite right,' Appleby said. 'Never miss out on the routine. Hard-won experience has created it.'

Ringwood received this with a moment's silence – possibly as detecting a hint of mockery in it. And then, suddenly, he smiled.

'Do you recall, sir,' he asked, 'saying a true word about this not a long time back? A kind of metaphor, I think they'd call it.'

'And now, Ringwood, you're producing a kind of riddle. What did I say?'

'You said, Sir John, that the key to the mystery lay in this confounded library.'

14

Bagot – perhaps after some token consultation with the bereaved Lady Osprey – had decided that luncheon should be a buffet affair. It was probably his view that, whatever the police might think, the house-party at Clusters had lasted long enough, and that a hint of imminent dispersal was in order. Such a hint might be given if the guests were required to remain on their feet as they munched, unless they were willing to perch on chairs ranged round the circumference of the room as at a ball. As this latter disposition would have been absurd, everybody remained perpendicular, including Lady Osprey herself in a slightly bewildered way – until, indeed, her son, furiously scowling, dragged forward one of the ranked chairs and made her sit on it.

Sir John Appleby, gnawing the while at a smoked salmon sandwich of the more obstinately stringy sort, didn't fail to remark this filial attention on Adrian Osprey's part, and he had a sense of it as obscurely significant. The young man's temperament appeared to be such that he might have been a little more than a shade rough with a girl, but he didn't somehow seem likely to have behind him the role of a patricide.

But Appleby faced another and less speculative consideration. Given that Lord Osprey's murder had been committed by the mysterious and alarming intruder at the French window of the library not many hours before the fatality, nobody now in the enjoyment of Bagot's buffet could qualify as the perpetrator. For when the intruder had briefly revealed himself to Lord Osprey and Miss Minnychip, the entire company had been congregated on the wrong side of the window, having gathered in the library for the purpose of imbibing what Adrian clearly regarded as the strikingly unsatisfactory family sherry.

And now the company was complete once more, since Marcus Broadwater had turned up from his river. Entering a little late, he had addressed a word or two to his sister – of too casual a sort, Appleby felt, to be quite appropriate to the occasion. And now he had turned to Appleby himself.

'Uncommonly annoying,' he said. 'Everything upset as a result of last night's revolting butchery. They even forgot to put a bite to eat in my basket. But, as it happened, the trout haven't been rising, anyway. Too much bright sunlight, I expect. Probably I'll go back and flog the water for an hour or two in the late afternoon. Perhaps I'll try a Poly May Dun. Any progress here?'

'You must ask the police,' Appleby said, and then abandoned so patently disingenuous a response. 'Ringwood has sent one or two things for forensic investigation, but I don't myself expect the results to be much of a surprise. Your brother-in-law was killed with a weapon snatched from one of those trophies on the library wall. That doesn't, to my own mind, suggest much in the way of premeditation. And we find that somebody has had out a little boat from the shed on the other side of the moat. That seems to tie in with the fellow fleetingly seen last night through the French window in the library. I don't know that there's anything more concrete than that.'

'Such as your information is, Sir John, it is good of you to give me word of it. And I am afraid I spoke to you rather foolishly this morning. Perhaps I was taken a little by surprise, my mind being already on the fish. I mean about being a good suspect, and so on.'

'I don't know that I took you very seriously, Mr Broadwater. By the way, does the name Minnychip count for much in the numismatic world?'

'Meaning our friend's late father?' Broadwater laughed good-naturedly. 'He was an Anglo-Indian of some sort, who interested himself in coinage from that point of vantage. I know that he contributed a number of well-informed articles to scholarly journals. And according to his daughter – as you have no doubt heard from the lady – he formed his own collection of coins from the Orient.'

'Would it be as important as the Osprey Collection?'

'Good Lord, no!' Broadwater was amused.

'Do you think Miss Minnychip herself knows much about coins in any sort of learned way? Or continues her father's interest by dealing in them – anything of that sort? Or ever betrays what might be regarded as an obsession with the subject?'

Broadwater accorded this string of questions a moment's thought.

'I'd scarcely suppose anything of the kind,' he then said. 'And she has never, by the way, invited me to take a look at what she has. That is perhaps a shade odd. And yet, why should she? Have you, incidentally, talked at all to Honoria Wimpole?'

'Not so far. But I take her to be the young woman standing by the fireplace.'

'Quite right. Now she is a numismatist. Another ten years, and she will be one of the leading authorities in our field. Curious, in a way. Her mother – talking to Quickfall, over there – is an uncommonly silly woman. Even as women go.'

Appleby made no comment on Broadwater's final remark here. But after another moment he asked a further question.

'Will Miss Wimpole have seen the Osprey Collection?'

'I don't know. But I imagine not. She may have come to Clusters in the hope of doing so.'

'The police still don't know where the Osprey Collection is kept. And you told me earlier this morning that you don't know either. That struck me as most extraordinary, and it still does. Ringwood was equally surprised when I passed on your information. And rather perturbed, really. Because it does seem not altogether unlikely that there is some link between your brother-in-law's death and this uncommonly elusive collection. It's almost as if – and you must forgive me for putting the point in this way

– with that death, you are the only person who knows positively that the coins exist.'

'That, Sir John – and now *you* must forgive *me* – is total nonsense. Over the years, a number of scholars of undeniable integrity have enjoyed the privilege of examining the Osprey Collection.'

'I don't doubt that for a moment, Mr Broadwater. And I must emend the point I was trying to make. You are now the only person who can possibly tell whether the Osprey Collection still exists in its integrity.'

'Only a couple of years ago my brother-in-law and I compiled and printed for private circulation a catalogue of the Osprey Collection. When the coins are found – as I hope they soon will be – the continued integrity of the collection can be checked against it.'

'The degree of collaboration between you which that entails seems to make all the odder the fact that you don't know the collection's whereabouts. It *will* have to be found, you know – if only for the probate people. Of course, there's that key.'

'Key?' Broadwater repeated sharply. His tone perhaps indicated a growing knowledge that this was scarcely a friendly interrogation.

'Ringwood and I found a key, rather oddly sited, in the library only an hour ago. I have taken it into my head that it may be the key to whatever secure place Lord Osprey kept his coins in. A small room or a cupboard: that sort of thing. Ringwood has a man going round with the key now – and instructions to try it wherever he sees a keyhole.'

'An unoccupied keyhole, I presume.'

'Well, I don't suppose the fellow will take much for granted. But – for a start, at least – he'll stick to the ground floor, because of Osprey's habit of parading his coins on a trolley. You must recall telling me about that this morning. By the way, did anybody else ever see him so oddly engaged?'

'I've no idea. But it would be reasonable to suppose that Bagot did. Bagot sees everything.'

'Even where the trolley and the collection came from?'

'I wouldn't go so far as to assert that, Sir John. Poor Oliver had a certain cunning to him. He was always something of an eccentric, you know. And that sort of thing was growing on him with the years. You must have noticed it yourself?'

'I scarcely knew your brother-in-law, Mr Broadwater. But I certainly never thought of him as cunning, or even eccentric.'

'In fact, Sir John, you only thought of him as slightly pompous and slightly boring. Well, the poor chap was those things as well. But *de mortuis nil nisi bonum*. May I get you a glass of wine?'

Appleby accepted the wine. It turned out to be burgundy – the same, presumably, that Bagot in his pantry had set to breathe earlier that morning. Appleby retired with his glass to a corner of the room, and there, undisturbed for a few minutes, achieved a synoptic view of the whole company. It depressed him, and he wondered why. Was it perhaps because he suddenly sensed all these people as starkly irrelevant to the problem on hand? Was the Osprey Collection itself a kind of mute irrelevance? It had first surfaced as a fragment of quite idle talk between Judith and himself on their way home from Clusters a few days previously. He had himself mentioned it to Ringwood in the course of his telephone conversation that morning, saying that its existence perhaps enhanced the possibility that attempted theft or burglary might be a factor in the mystery. Almost immediately after that it had figured prominently in the course of his bizarre encounter with Marcus Broadwater when he was obeying Lady Osprey's summons to Clusters. Immediately after that again there had been his meeting with the local clergyman, Mr Brackley; and with Brackley he had himself at once raised the topic of the coins. It might almost be said that they had now become an obsession with him: since the moment of his arrival at Clusters they had never for long been out of his head.

But was the Osprey Collection a mere will-o'-the-wisp – not as simply being without substantial existence (although, indeed, he was still without solid proof that it *did* exist) but as bearing the character of a small, delusive flame the sole effect of which was to lead one hopelessly astray? Had the murder of Lord Osprey (for that he had been murdered was – except indeed for Bagot with his absurd notion of an accident – the one solid fact in the affair so far) been the consequence of some situation with which the unfortunate man's hoard of ancient coins had no connection?

Appleby paused on this, as his training had taught him to do. When in doubt or at a stand, step back and attempt a little radical rethinking, a totally fresh approach. Above all, when you have a murdered man on your hands, *find out about him.*

So what did he know about Lord Osprey? What sort of picture of the owner of Clusters had he brought to Clusters with him, and in what particulars had he added to it since? The answers to these questions proved, on scrutiny, to be thoroughly unsatisfactory. On some fairly recent occasion television had given him a glimpse of Lord Osprey making a speech in the House of Lords, and had even afforded him a brief snippet of it. On the strength of this he had concluded that nature had not intended the man to be a legislator, and he had even described him to Judith as a political ignoramus. This had been hasty and intolerant, and it was possible to see another side to the picture. Osprey was a hereditary peer, not one of those citizens who have become 'life' peers as the result of a long frequentation of public affairs. And a majority of hereditary peers seldom or never go near the House of Lords, believing it to be an obsolete or at least tiresome institution. A few may attend and speak there out of vanity – but not many, since the majority have ample means of satisfying vanity in other directions. Those who do attend and take part in the work of the House are, on the whole, to be described

as conscientious if sometimes not particularly talented persons. Osprey had probably
belonged with these. What could be said
with some certainty was that he had not
been a highly intelligent man: to pursue, as
he appeared to have done, a hobby of which
he had gained very little command was
surely definitive on the point.

But what about him in his social relations,
and as a family man? Here, Appleby realized
that he knew almost nothing. There had
been that luncheon party, with its talk of bats
in the belfry. He had carried away from it an
impression of the Ospreys as not much
interested in their guests, nor in one another,
either. Osprey had been a little inclined to
brow-beat his wife, but this didn't seem to
have bothered her. There was no sort of
tension between them, and perhaps there
never had been. It was possible to wonder
how they had ever come to get married,
particularly as they seemed to stem from
somewhat disparate backgrounds. This
morning, what might be called the blankness
of Lady Osprey's response to her sudden
and shocking widowhood suggested that the
relationship between husband and wife
wasn't and never had been other than on the
shallow side. Nor did Adrian, their only

child, seem to set much store on family ties. He was perhaps a little more attached to his mother than to his father, but he hadn't struck Appleby as a young man who had grown up much nourished by the domestic affections. The entire picture was rather dull, with no strong accent anywhere to be discerned in it. Perhaps there was some-where such an accent, but of a kind kept by general consent distinctly under drapes.

This was all very unsatisfactory and vague, and it would perhaps be best to keep the Osprey Collection and its riddle at, as it were, the centre of the composition. Appleby had almost arrived at this conclusion when the preserved decorum of Bagot's buffet was broken in upon by a sudden and totally un-expected occasion of scandal and confusion.

15

The disturbance began with a clamour emanating from the main Entrance Hall of Clusters which has already been described, and the effect was of that lofty and marble sheathed oval as abruptly given over to disgrace and spoliation at the hands of an insurgent mob. Just so might some great cathedral have resounded to the destructive frenzy of a wandering barbarian horde. One might have imagined the non-existent statues in their vacant niches as looking on helpless and aghast at mounting chaos. Much of this was acoustic delusion, but what immediately succeeded upon it was even more alarming. The bivalvular doors of the apartment in which the assembled gentlefolk were recruiting themselves burst open, and, almost filling the wide space thus created, there appeared an enormous man, red-faced, glaring, and bellowing furiously. For a moment he stood motionless, confronting the company. Then he turned half round, seized a young woman who had been cowering behind him, and propelled her in front of him into the room.

'Where is he?' the enormous man shouted. 'Show me the ruddy bastard! I'll learn him, I will. I'll leave him so that he won't want to do it again – or be able to, if I get my hands on him you know where. Bloody aristocratic ripper!'

From behind this volcanically eruptive person there appeared the pale face of Bagot. Bagot was clearly frightened out of his wits – but even so, his duty to uphold the covenances momentarily sustained him.

'Mr Trumfitt and Miss Trumfitt, my lady,' he announced, and thereupon bolted from view.

Mr Trumfitt pausing to take breath, there was a moment's stupefied silence – into which, however, snivelling noises were interjected by his daughter. So here – Appleby thought – were the outraged publican from a local village and his ravished daughter. Obscurely, he drew a certain encouragement from this. For some little time the situation had been unpromisingly static. Here at least was development. It was, of course, awkward for Adrian. But you can't be a bit rough with village girls and expect always to get away with it.

'Where's his lordship?' Trumfitt yelled. 'Where's that bloody Lord Osprey? I'll put my hands on him, I will. You'll all see if I won't.' He glared round the company. 'Crawled into the woodwork, has he? I'll have him out of it.'

There was another moment's silence, and then Adrian stepped forward.

'I am Lord Osprey,' he said. 'What do you want with me?'

'You bloody little brat, get back to school!' Trumfitt shouted. And he turned to his daughter. 'Avice,' he said, 'tell them all it wasn't the young one.'

'No more it weren't,' Avice said. 'And he's not a lord yet, he isn't.' And with a certain dramatic sense, Avice turned to the company at large. 'It were the old un,' she said. 'And where is he? My dad has promised to hold him down while I get my nails in him.'

At this point several of the guests had sufficiently recovered from their surprise – and fright – to utter disapproving noises. But the first to speak was Rupert Quickfall.

'This is most unseemly,' he said. 'Why have these persons been admitted to the house – let alone allowed to pass half a dozen police-men?'

'But I think that some explanation should

be given us.' Lady Wimpole, although obviously much confused in mind, spoke with surprising emphasis. 'Certainly those horrible people ought to be taken away. But what does the young woman mean by saying that Adrian isn't yet a peer? And what does this disgusting man mean by demanding to see Adrian's father?' Alarm now sounded in Lady Wimpole's voice. 'Poor Oliver *is* dead, isn't he?'

'Really, Mama, this is too absurd.' It was Honoria who now spoke. 'Of course Lord Osprey is dead – only this man, who seems to have some grudge against him, hasn't heard of the fact.'

'Dead!' shouted Trumfitt on a note of outraged incredulity. 'Of course he isn't dead – not yet, he isn't. It's a trick. Smuggling him out of the country to escape appearing in the dock. That's what they're up to. I'll have the law on the lot of them.'

'The law is sometimes an ass,' Appleby said. 'But not quite to that extent, perhaps. Quickfall, have you anything to say about all this?'

'My dear Appleby, if a touch of the facetious weren't out of place before a mess-up of the present sort, I'd be inclined to say that I reserve my defence. Clearly I got things a little the wrong way round on the telephone. The generations got themselves slightly mixed up. For the moment, I'll rest on that.'

'I don't think anybody ought to rest.' This came from a lady whom Appleby identified provisionally as the shadowy Mrs Purvis, wife of one of the Purvises of Purvis, Purvis and Purvis. 'We are in a perfectly shocking situation,' Mrs Purvis went on. 'No sooner is Lord Osprey brutally murdered than we are publicly confronted with some disgusting aspersion upon him. We ought all to bestir ourselves, and begin by supporting Lady Osprey and her son in any way we can.'

'Quite right!' Miss Minnychip spoke in her turn. 'Poor Oliver is dead, and – so far as the law goes – he can, I suppose, be slandered with impunity. But of slander we can at least express our detestation. Many have fallen by the edge of the sword: but not so many as have fallen by the tongue.'

'Thank you, my dear.' Lady Osprey, in order to utter these very proper words, appeared to have to contend with a certain absence of mind. She was still sitting on the chair Adrian had provided for her, and she had perhaps been reflecting, Appleby thought, on the disposition of articles of furniture in the dower house. For one whose husband had been murdered and then within twenty-four hours apparently aspersed as a ravisher Lady Osprey seemed to own just the right temperament.

'What about having in those policemen?' Mr Purvis asked abruptly. 'Sir John, wouldn't they be just right for dealing with our unwelcome visitors?'

'I think I'd rather have Mr Trumfitt and his daughter leave quietly and of their own free will,' Appleby said. 'Mr Broadwater, what do you think about that?'

'I rather agree, Sir John.' Marcus Broadwater had been the only one of the company not to speak so far. 'It's my opinion that they are conceivably not being wholly candid with us. But if they are willing to go, let them go. For one thing – but I defer to Quickfall here – once an intruder has gained entry to a private property, the law about getting him out again is surprisingly tricky. He has to be guilty of threatening behaviour, or something of that sort, before the police can bundle him out of the door and into a van.'

'But we've all heard Mr Trumfitt going for threatening behaviour in a big way. Emasculation, and nothing short of it, was what he appears to have been envisaging.'

'But that threat, Sir John, was directed against a man who is in fact dead: the late Lord Osprey. The present Lord Osprey was merely enjoined to go back to school. That was what the law is, no doubt, prepared to call vulgar abuse. But I doubt whether it can be construed as a threat.'

These learned exchanges were interrupted by Mr Trumfitt himself. He had been surprisingly silent for more than five minutes. Now he began roaring again. His daughter, as if taking a cue from this, resumed her snivelling. Appleby failed to discern in her any suggestion of a maidenhood but lately wronged. He had to remind himself of Quickfall's undeniably valid assertion that a drab is as entitled as a duchess to resist the violent embraces of a male.

And then, if only briefly, Adrian Osprey took charge of the situation, directly confronting the enraged publican.

'Mr Trumfitt,' he said, 'my father is dead. There is every reason to believe that he has been murdered. And you are creating a disgraceful scene. Please go away, and take your daughter with you.'

This firm speech was surprisingly effective. Mr Trumfitt grabbed the blubbering Avice and dragged her to the door. But there he turned, and gave a final shout at the company.

'I'll be even with the whole pack of you!' he roared. After which – and presumably unaware that he had thus closely paraphrased a celebrated line in Shakespeare – he bundled both Avice and himself out of the room.

16

It speaks well for the resilience of the upper reaches of English society that after this vulgar irruption upon Bagot's buffet the company picked itself up at once and assumed every appearance of undisturbed polite life. Bagot himself assisted this recovery by bringing in coffee and gravely handing it round with the assistance of a parlour maid. And Appleby assisted too – at least to the extent of deftly grabbing a sugar basin and crossing the room in order to offer it to Honoria Wimpole, introducing himself as he did so. Honoria was amused.

'I know about you,' she said, 'and believe you want to pump me. Pump away.'

'I want to know about coins, really, Miss Wimpole. Apart from Mr Broadwater – with whom I have already had a good deal of talk – you are the only numismatist here.'

'Not really. There's Miss Minnychip, Sir John.'

'She is a guardian of such things, but I don't think she knows – or claims to know –

a great deal about them. She simply treasures a collection made by her father. I mustn't tell you where she keeps it – although I can say that its whereabouts reflect a keen sense of its worth. Is the Minnychip Collection, as it may be called, really of the first importance?'

'I scarcely think one can say that of it. But it has its strengths, I believe. Slender coins from Assyria and thick ones from Latium. Tablets of Bactriana. Bull, star, globe, crescent, and so on. All attractively named for amateurs. Who could resist *zianies?* They're things minted by the Moors in a gold alloy.'

'And every one of them worth ten *reales.*'

'Sir John, I've been showing off, and now you're making fun of me. You must be something of a numismatist yourself.'

'Far from it. I've simply read *Don Quixote.* But, for the moment, let's forget about Miss Minnychip. Of course it's the Osprey Collection that's in every way important now. Have you had a sight of it?'

'No, I have not, Sir John. Nor many other people either, so far as I can make out. But there's been a catalogue.'

'I know about that. Are you here because you hoped to be given sight of it?'

'Yes.'

'But you haven't been?'

'No.'

'But you were still hoping, right up to this nasty affair?'

'Certainly I was. I came here with my mother because Lord Osprey had more or less promised to show me his collection.'

'But he didn't?'

'No. I've already said that, haven't I? Today or tomorrow, it would have happened, I think. We were getting on rather well together, Lord Osprey and I.'

'Did he tell you where the Osprey Collection was kept?'

'Kept, Sir John?'

'He made a secret of it, it seems. He didn't divulge it to you?'

'Definitely not. I imagine it must be in some sort of strong room. It is extremely valuable. Its nature makes it that. It's not like, say, a great Mantegna or Turner, the direct market value of which, to a thief, is nil. Coins can be sent all over the place, and simply sold piecemeal. Ideal booty, in fact.'

'Worth committing murder for?'

'Most definitely. And that's what has happened, I suppose.'

'I don't know that we can yet be quite sure of that, Miss Wimpole. And may I now venture on more delicate ground?'

'Yes, you may. And I know what's in your head, Sir John. The reach of the late Lord Osprey's amorous proclivities.'

'Well, yes.' This was going a little fast for Sir John Appleby, an elderly and therefore misdoubting spectator of a much younger generation. 'The territory we seemed to be hearing about from that Mr Trumfitt.'

'Quite so. And you want to know whether I tried softening up Lord Osprey through an exhibition of female charm.'

'Stuff and nonsense, Miss Wimpole. You wouldn't need to put on any turn in order to be attractive to this wretched dead man. My question is simply whether you judged him to be on the inflammable side?'

'As in this story about Miss Trumfitt? Very probably, I'd say. But he was also prepared to doat, which isn't quite the same thing.'

'I'm not sure that I follow you, Miss Wimpole.'

'By doating I mean a kind of flirting to no practical intent in what he perfectly well knew to be a no-go area. It's tiresome to have to admit to such a thing as going on in one's own frosty cabbage patch. But I did let him doat, and thereby got a little nearer to the Osprey Collection.' Honoria Wimpole paused on this. 'He wasn't, by the way, altogether a stupid man. And that cut down my feeling of false pretences. I mean that he knew perfectly well that, even if he poured his every treasure on my head – owls from Athens, winged horses from Corinth, turtles from Aegina – it wouldn't bring us an inch nearer together. He doated, all right. But there was always a groat's worth of wit in his pate.'

'Can you cite an instance of that?'

'His putting up with Marcus Broadwater. Broadwater seems to me to have been a thoroughly tiresome brother-in-law. But at some point or other Lord Osprey had the wit to spot him as a godsend.'

'Explain.'

'I'm afraid you'll find it rather fanciful. I seem to see Lord Osprey as one of nature's misers – and in a quite pathological way. Discovering in himself an impulse to conceal small bags of money in secure hiding-places all over this enormous house. That sort of thing.'

'It's an ingenious thought, Miss Wimpole. Go on.'

'But he had sense enough to fear that, if he carried that to an extreme, his family would be worried, and doctors called in, and in no time he'd find himself put under trustees or even carted away as a lunatic. And then he found the expedient of hiding not current coins but ancient ones. And having realized that this would be judged a perfectly respectable activity, and that he had a brother-in-law in a position to advise him and at the same time to cover his own almost complete ignorance of numismatics, he started up what we now call the Osprey Collection. What do you think, Sir John?'

'I think that you yourself, in becoming a professional numismatist, cheated the world of a very promising novelist.'

'But doesn't my theory – well, *fit*? All this concealment of where the Osprey Collection is kept: what's that if it isn't miserhood?'

'You have a point or two there, Miss Wimpole. Broadwater says that he himself has been kept in ignorance of the collection's whereabouts – and that, to my mind, is a striking dottiness in itself. But I'm not at all sure of its helping me to solve the mystery of Lord Osprey's murder. And that's the job I seem to have taken on. I'm at Clusters as a policeman – retired, but still a bit of a policeman and not as an alienist.'

'And my discovery – because I'm convinced it's that – takes us a long way from

Mr Trumfitt and his daughter.'

'It does seem so. But I'm not quite sure of the irrelevance, as one may call it, of the Trumfitt dimension.'

'But, Sir John, you must at least admit that Trumfitt is not the murderer. For here he was, less than an hour ago, roaring and thirsting for Lord Osprey's blood.'

'Again you have a point, Miss Wimpole. But I'm not quite sure that it is a conclusive one. And if we go back to the theme of what you have called Lord Osprey's amorous proclivities, there's the odd fact that Mr Quickfall – who must normally be pretty clear-headed to have got where he has as a barrister – managed to believe that it was Adrian, and not Adrian's father – who disgraced himself in relation to the lovely Avice Trumfitt.'

Appleby paused on this, quite aware that he had produced something of a *non sequitur*, but watching Honoria keenly as he spoke. And the young woman instantly flushed with anger.

'Disgusting nonsense!' she said. 'And if Quickfall believed he was told anything of the sort, it must have been because he was thoroughly fuddled at the time. And he looks to me as if he drinks like a fish.'

'The notion of Adrian as a crude ravisher is utterly alien to the young man's character?'

'Of course it is. I don't care tuppence for Adrian Osprey' – and Honoria's flush deepened as she spoke – 'but he isn't in the least that sort of person.'

Appleby accepted this with a nod. He had the habit of taking satisfaction in making discoveries, whether relevant to some matter in hand, or not.

'May I just take up one further point?' he asked. 'It's rather a crude one, I'm afraid – but murder mysteries often have to move that way. It's just about the pounds and pence aspect of the thing. Or perhaps the dollars and cents. You have seen that privately printed catalogue; studied it pretty carefully, I don't doubt. So can you put an approximate value on the Osprey Collection?'

'By value, Sir John, I suppose you mean something like brute cost – what the Osprey Collection might be expected to fetch at the fall of the hammer?'

'Exactly that. Call it an auctioneer's estimate.'

'It's something not at all simple to arrive at.' Honoria glanced at Appleby in what might have been taken as mild amusement. 'There are private collectors in America, you know, who might either turn up or stay away. There might even be a Saudi prince or two, with a large whack of the world's oil revenues at command. One of these people might be a *mad* collector. Even a couple of them might be that. And the parties might all favour a private deal to a public auction. Lord Osprey himself would have done so, provided he was at all well advised. A little man like that Purvis could explain the point to him at once. Lord Osprey, you see, no doubt guided by Marcus Broadwater, will have been fairly active in the auction rooms himself over the last few years at least. So in the eyes of the Inland Revenue any auction he authorized would rank as one in a series of transactions – and to anything that can be so represented very heavy taxation applies. It's a situation – as you can well imagine – that conduces to the engineering of quiet private deals. And collectors – private collectors at least – are particularly attracted to that if they *are* a little loco, as many are. Which is a long-winded way of saying that your question is a non-question. There's no answer to it.'

'But some sort of side-glance, perhaps? I'd like to hear you actually name a sum of money.'

'Very well.' And Honoria reflected for a moment. 'Go back to Miss Minnychip's Anglo-Indian papa, and consider the kind of coins he was in a particular position to collect. For example, the East India Company's *mohurs* struck in silver. In a strict numismatic regard, they're of very little interest. And aesthetically considered, they're not all that. But the other day I heard of one – minted, I think, in 1854 or thereabouts – knocked down for about £2,000. It's annoying, really, if one happens to be on the side of the major public collections.'

Sir John Appleby, thus rather ruthlessly and at length taught his *ABC*, laughed good-humouredly.

'I should have thought of all that,' he said. 'Can I get you another cup of coffee? No? Then I think I'll go and have a word with my colleague Ringwood. But thank you very much.'

17

Having thus formally re-enlisted himself, as it were, in the police force, Appleby made his way back to the Music Saloon. Ringwood was there, and came to him at once.

'Having lunch with the nobs, Sir John?' The Detective-Inspector had clearly taken a liking to the eminently tactful veteran. 'I went to a local pub, and had what they call a ploughman's lunch. Bread and cheese and beer, but no ploughmen present. There were several locals of one sort or another, however, and I managed to have a word with them. They hadn't, of course, heard about Lord Osprey's death. Incidentally, the pub is called The Osprey Arms. It always strikes me as odd, how many pot-houses are named like that. You'd think the relevant armigerous grandees would object.'

'They never seem to have objected, and I suppose the thing was taken to add to their consequence. They used even to like having their arms engraved on milestones. Did you manage to have a word with the licensee?'

'He didn't seem to be around. But I noticed his name over the door, and heard a bit about him. Trumfitt.'

'Trumfitt it would be, and he was here, paying what might be termed a morning call.' And Appleby briefly sketched the untoward incident at luncheon. 'Did you hit on any relevant talk?' he then asked.

'I gathered something that may be very relevant, in the light of what you've just told me, Sir John. Despite his years, Lord Osprey seems to have been a bit of a lad. That was the expression. It seemed to mean that he interested himself from time to time in village girls.'

'Relevant, indeed. Did you gather anything about Trumfitt?'

'Careful about his licence. A third pint the limit. And if a man gets really stroppy, out he goes on his ear. Trumfitt must have a strong arm and a quick temper.'

'He wasn't exactly being careful about his licence, Ringwood, here at Clusters less than an hour ago. Storming into this stately home, and bellowing, more or less, for its proprietor's blood, is scarcely the way to keep in with a bench of local magistrates.' Appleby considered this for a moment. 'Do you know,' he said, 'I think I'm wrong there?

If Lord Osprey wasn't much admired by the gentry of the county – if they thought of him as rather a pompous and boring fellow who didn't always behave himself with young women – they might be inclined to give Trumfitt quite a good mark for the show he put up here. By the way, did you gather whether there's a Mrs Trumfitt?'

'There isn't. She died a couple of years ago.'

'How very odd! I mean, Ringwood, how remarkable that you should have extracted such information over a pint of beer in The Osprey Arms.'

'I didn't, Sir John. It's just my habit to take a stroll through any country churchyard that comes my way. And there she was. Beloved wife and mother, and so on.'

'God bless my soul, Ringwood! It's the sort of habit that Conan Doyle might have planted on Sherlock Holmes. But what about the lovely Avice? Did you hear anything about her when you were in the pub?'

'I did hear a little. She helps regularly in the bar, and is much admired by the yokels. But, again, they have to mind their Ps and Qs. A bit of lip to the girl, and out you go.'

'A jealous and zealous and hot-tempered papa. It all fits in with the exhibition we had here. An irrelevant side-show, at a guess. But I'm bound to say it bobs up uncommonly pat.'

'When one is guessing, Sir John, I suppose it's a sign one ought to be trying to find out more. In whatever the area in question may be, that is.'

'You're absolutely right, Ringwood, and we mustn't simply let Trumfitt pass by. Suppose we go the whole hog and swear to ourselves that it was this infuriated publican who killed Lord Osprey. Just what difficulties do we face?'

'For a start, Sir John, there's his having turned up here in the way he did, not an hour ago. What do we say about that?'

'We say that it's an instance of the very common phenomenon of the guilty man returning to haunt the scene of his crime. But to that we have to add what may be called an element of primitive deception. Trumfitt, dragging the unfortunate Avice along with him, burst into Clusters more or less howling for Lord Osprey's blood. And you don't howl for the blood of a man you've already killed. So by putting on today's turn he felt he was distancing himself from his last night's murder. So far, it's plain sailing. But what other difficulties do we face, Ringwood?'

'The possibility of alibi, Sir John. Actually, of two alibis. The dinner-hour here at Clusters seems to be eight o'clock. So it was round about half past seven that there was that appearance at the library window. That's well past opening time at a pub. Was Trumfitt on view behind his bar at that hour? It's a crucial question, and one not too difficult to get an answer to. I can have one of my men get into plain clothes, take himself off to the public bar at The Osprey Arms this evening, and raise hell by swearing he was short changed there at the same hour yesterday. It will at once become evident whether Trum-fitt was then in charge of things or not.'

'Excellent – and that's the crucial point in the way of alibi. The other one doesn't pack much punch. Osprey seems to have been killed around about midnight, or in the small hours. A widower can't be expected to provide witnesses to his whereabouts at such a time. But there is another question I'd like to get settled. Do you know? I think you and I ought to have a further word with that fellow Bagot.'

The butler was discovered in his pantry, recruiting himself against any further stresses the day might bring by a leisured ingestion of sandwiches and burgundy. Appleby found himself thinking rather well of Bagot – at least in point of his professional character. Clusters was a rambling anachronism, an outmoded machine rusty in some parts, in others distinctly in need of oil, or fined away by friction in areas where replacements would be distinctly hard to find. And amid all this Bagot clearly had the function of a tireless escapement, an insignificant part of the whole, but one entirely dedicated to maintaining the appearance of an orderly progression of hour upon hour and day upon day. Appleby, who was inwardly still a little resentful at having got himself caught up in the messy business of Lord Osprey's sudden decease, was abruptly aware in himself of a freakish wish that it should be Bagot who would finally be unmasked as the villain of the piece. In popular fiction butlers, although in real life of a race almost as extinct as the dodo, were still constantly coming upon slaughtered employers in libraries. Why not, for a change, a butler who had himself done the deed? Had anyone thought of that? Appleby, who had read singularly few detective stories, didn't at all know. Certainly the present situation at Clusters held small promise in this direction. Almost everything in the set-up would have to be drastically rearranged if anything of the sort were to be achieved.

All this was a most culpable vagary on Appleby's part, and as its consequence Detective-Inspector Ringwood was for the moment left to make all the running. As Ringwood was without any clear notion of why this visit to the butler's pantry was being made, a certain sense of inconsequence not unnaturally ensued. And it was contributed to by Bagot himself, who quite failed to exhibit his customary poise in the presence of his callers. This was perhaps a matter of social confusion. Bagot knew precisely how to comport himself with Sir John Appleby. He had a fairly clear notion of what would be proper with a detective-inspector, who could be thought of as roughly equivalent to a regimental sergeant-major. The obscure factor lay in the relationship between his two visitors, an understanding of which must necessarily condition his own current bearing to each. This shadowy punctilio amused Appleby, who had the hang of it. Ringwood, sensing it more obscurely, was impatient and annoyed.

'Bagot,' Ringwood said abruptly, 'Sir John has a point or two to put to you.'

'It's chiefly this, Mr Bagot,' Appleby said. 'Just what do we know about that fellow Trumfitt and his daughter? They made a shocking row, I must say.'

'Most disgraceful, Sir John. I ought not to have announced them. I regret announcing them. Only I knew, of course, that you were among those taking luncheon, and I felt that you could deal effectively with the incident.'

This was so disingenuous as to be, to Appleby's thinking, almost endearing. Bagot had 'announced' the Trumfitts because the roaring publican had put him in a blind funk. And some of the guests had been almost equally alarmed. Of the company surprised while nibbling their sandwiches and sipping their burgundy it had been Adrian Osprey who had best measured up to the irruption.

'And of course,' Bagot went on, 'her ladyship has always insisted that no former employee should be turned from the door.'

'Former employee!' Ringwood interposed sharply. 'Just what do you mean by that, my man?'

Bagot (who was properly 'Mr Bagot' to

anybody other than members of the Osprey family and their most intimate friends) clearly and justly felt 'my man' to be an outrage. He signified the fact by turning to Appleby in a kind of expectant silence. So Appleby took up the running again.

'Are you telling Mr Ringwood and myself,' he asked, 'that this pub keeper once had a job here at Clusters?'

'Certainly, Sir John.'

'Some time ago?'

'Thirty years back, it would be.'

'But within your own recollection?'

'Certainly, sir. It was in the late Lord Osprey's time.' Bagot saw there might be an ambiguity in this. 'The former Lord Osprey, Sir John. I was myself still in livery, and getting a little restless that way. The then Lady Osprey had a fancy for tall footmen, so my six feet were something of a disadvantage to me. But I did become his lordship's butler a few years later. Nowadays, Sir John, I almost feel myself to have held the position man and boy. Man and boy, Sir John, and seeing Lord Ospreys come and go. It's what makes the present tragedy so affecting to me.'

Appleby nodded sympathetically, and Ringwood hastened to follow suit.

'So Trumfitt, Mr Bagot, would have been

under you?'

'Not at all, Sir John. I have, I fear, given you quite a wrong impression of his standing. He was simply one of the outside men. There were about a dozen of them at that time. We gave them a meal – although not, of course, in the servants' hall – but they slept above the stables, and in places like that.'

'So you had no very close contact with young Trumfitt, Mr Bagot.' Appleby had settled down into a tone of relaxed chat. 'Was he one of the outside men for many years? We seem to be talking about matters a long time back.'

'For about five years, I'd say, he worked at Clusters. A strong lad, and willing enough. But with a quick temper to him, that at times had him getting on with the others none too well. In the end they ganged up on him, some of them did.'

'Violence, was there?'

'He found himself in the moat, Sir John – or in the deep mud that passed for the moat in places, then as now. After that, I believe he went for a soldier. But the late Lord Osprey – him that now lies dead that is – remembered what the other lads had done against him all those years back, and he put in a word for him when he came looking for that public house. Without, I'd say, any inquiry into the way Trumfitt's character had been developing.'

'You give us a very coherent account of the matter, Mr Bagot. We're obliged to you.' It might have been a much younger and rather artlessly artful Appleby who produced this. 'Just what sort of work would young Trumfitt have been doing as a lad here? Grooming the horses – that sort of thing?'

'By no means, Sir John.' Bagot appeared mildly shocked. 'The horses – hunters, of course, for the most part – were important at Clusters in those days, and it was trained men who looked after them. Young Trumfitt was simply one of the head gardener's lads – and would be set, as likely as not, weeding between the flags in the great court, with nothing but a broken knife from the kitchens to help him. That, or skimming the duckweed from the moat. Not work that any young man would take much satisfaction in, to my mind. It may well have given a twist in his character. A further twist, you may say, to what was already there.'

'You mean,' Ringwood asked, 'that Trumfitt was the kind that harbours grudges?'

'Just that. But mark you, Mr Inspector, we never heard ill of him during these later years in that public house – not until the disgraceful scene that blew up here not an hour ago. But when I opened the door to him and his daughter I saw at once there was something amiss with him. I blame myself for letting him enter. I repeat that.'

'Were you frightened of him?' Ringwood asked.

'No doubt I shared in the general perturbation.' Bagot made this admission with dignity. 'Sir John would not have been alarmed. And her ladyship appears, not unnaturally, to be suffering considerable absences of mind, and perhaps scarcely knew what was going on.'

'Did you gather just what was going on – what sort of assertion this Trumfitt was making?'

'Certainly, Inspector. I need hardly say that I heard nothing of what was said after I announced those persons and withdrew. But the man Trumfitt had already made himself tolerably clear to me – outrageously so, indeed – while still in the hall. The young woman, too.'

'Well now, Bagot, what do you think about it? Was there anything in it? Can you provide any evidence about the imputation – either for or against it?'

But this was not the way to handle Bagot, as Appleby, silent for the moment, knew very well.

'As to that,' Bagot said, 'I have nothing to say. It wouldn't be proper – proper at all. Except,' he added – and it was rather as if he had remembered something read in a book or newspaper – 'in the presence of my solicitor.'

'Good God, man! Do you imagine you're going to be charged with anything?' Irritation had momentarily overcome discretion with Ringwood. 'Sir John, I'm in your hands.'

'Not at all, my dear chap. It's entirely your case.' Appleby thus hastened to obviate the threat of any unseemly friction between the two representatives of the law. 'And we must agree that Mr Bagot has been most helpful – as he can always be relied on to be. But now we're holding him up from his very responsible work. So we must simply thank him, and withdraw.'

'Sorry about that,' Ringwood said gruffly, as the two men walked down the corridor.

'Nonsense!' Appleby said, laughing. 'But in grand houses always butter up the servants. It was one of the things they said to me in my first probationary week in the CID.'

'I don't know that buttering up Bagot has taken us very far. Just where are we going now?'

'It looks like the Music Saloon, Ringwood, and your little posse of assistants with their gadgetry. They include one rather good-looking girl.'

'Do they, indeed, sir?' Ringwood asked this dryly, and clearly as one indisposed to frivolity. 'What I meant was about our progress in this affair. Would you say that Bagot has given us any sort of useful nudge along the way?'

'It depends on what you mean by the way, I suppose. If it's that underwater labyrinth that you and I encountered this morning, the answer is "Yes". We heard, for the first time, of somebody who had ample occasion to know his way about the moat.'

'Trumfitt?'

'Trumfitt long ago. The lad who, among other chores, pottered around in that little boat – or in a previous little boat – chasing up the duckweed. He's the first person we've heard of who, last night, could have got from any *A* to any *B* on that stinking anachronism without wasting time about it.'

'True enough, Sir John. But I don't know that it very clearly points to our precious pub keeper as a murderer. If you've slit a man's throat in the small hours, you don't come bellowing for his blood a few hours later.' Ringwood paused on this. 'Unless,' he at once soberly added, 'as a kind of bluff or blind. A bit primitive, that.'

'The possibility has occurred to me. And our friend Trumfitt doesn't strike me as a particularly sophisticated man.'

'Which wouldn't preclude his going hopping mad out of an outrage offered to his daughter. So Trumfitt's a suspect all right.'

'Certainly he is. He's that – but no more than that.'

'At least nothing to do with those bloody coins, Sir John.'

'Nothing whatever. But it's the coins that may be bloody – or blood-straked – all the same.'

'But Trumfitt remains, to say the least, something of an outsider in the race?'

'Definitely that. But in our sort of race, Ringwood, we have to keep an eye on the outsider right up to the winning post.'

'And that's a true word, Sir John.' Ringwood nodded sagely. 'The field is still open. Not a doubt about that.'

18

In the hall they ran into Mr Brackley. He offered both men a passing nod, but then came to a halt, as if feeling he must explain himself.

'I can't say "good afternoon",' he said, 'since no time ago I said "good morning" to each of you. When I got home there was a telephone call from our bereaved young man, asking me to come back and have a word with him. No doubt I ought to have thought of it in the first place, when I cycled over to see his mother.'

'I'd suppose it to have been his business to be present at that meeting,' Appleby said. 'Adrian will have to learn to consider the forms, will he not, now that he's the head of the family. And, without doubt, he is your leading parishioner.' This was an echo of a little joke Judith Appleby had made, but her husband had failed to remember the fact.

'I don't know I'd call him that myself, Sir John, unless in a moment of uncommon formality. For what is a parishioner? In essence what is he – or she? I'd say it's some-body who, at least occasionally, turns up in church. And I doubt whether Adrian Osprey has done that since – well, since they carried him to the font and he became Adrian.'

'He scarcely had a say in that, sir.' Rather surprisingly, Detective-Inspector Ringwood came out with this. 'It's not everybody who believes in infant baptism. John Baptist himself didn't make a kids' business of it, if the Gospels are to be believed.'

This unexpected emergence of the Voice of Dissent at once delighted the vicar of Little Clusters.

'My dear sir,' he said, 'we must talk about that. Just give me your address, and I'll call and have a chat. Yes, indeed!' And he turned to Appleby. 'First things first, Sir John – isn't that right?'

Thus abruptly confronted with the urgency of theological discussion, Appleby was momentarily put to a stand.

'Of course, I defer to you,' he then said. 'And I mustn't say that Lord Osprey's death is of the same importance as the problem of paedo-baptism. But it's important, all the same, and moreover getting to the bottom of it is urgent. I'm sure you agree. And pre-sumably it was what was in Adrian Osprey's mind when he asked you to come back to Clusters?'

'He certainly wants the mystery resolved. But his mother had been worrying over some practical matters, and he felt I might be a help with them. Whether, for instance, when a man has been murdered, the body can be buried before there's been an inquest. And about the reading of a will, and the like. Mr Ringwood, here, has a better sense of my proper territory. Adrian seemed to feel that such matters must come before me every week. I said what I could, and told him to send at once for the family solicitor. No doubt, that means some large firm in London. But they'll certainly have somebody here before the day is out.'

'Adrian didn't – but I don't know whether I ought to ask you this – he didn't strike you as anxious in any way to get something off his chest?'

'He said – and I think, Sir John, I can answer you readily enough – he said something about having been a bloody poor sort of son. It was, I think, no more than a general sense of inadequacy that was in question, and the worry must be accounted to his credit. It is true that he appears to be not an altogether easy youth. Or exactly a model son. But which of us, for that matter, has been that?'

'You have a true word there,' Ringwood said. It was to be presumed that Ringwood was a family man.

'This morning,' Appleby continued, 'you and I, Mr Brackley, exchanged a word or two about the Osprey Collection.'

'Ah, yes – the coins! I recall that.'

'Had Adrian anything to say about them; for instance, did he express any worry about their apparent elusiveness?'

'He made no mention of them, at all.'

'Or did he seem concerned about the financial consequences of his father's death?'

'Nothing of the kind seemed to be in his head.'

'I ask for several reasons. What is called, I think, capital transfer tax is now often a great worry to seemingly wealthy people. If an unexpected death occurs, severe headaches may result for the heirs. And I have a slight sense that Lord Osprey's affairs were not quite as he'd have wished them to be. From that fellow Purvis, indeed, he was fishing for the means to a little quick money. That's not of any great significance, I suppose. But there are other things it might be useful to know. The Osprey estate itself – meaning the landed estate – appears to be not all that considerable, and although there are a good many valuable things in this great barrack of a place, they mightn't add up to all that. So in what did Osprey's main wealth consist? Or, conceivably, does it not really exist? And that brings me back to those blessed coins. Are they possibly of sufficient value to be really important – even crucial – for the total financial set-up?'

'My dear Sir John!' The vicar seemed amused that this question should be put to him. 'It's hardly necessary to say that I am no authority on such things. But, at a guess, I'd regard it as very improbable that the coins rate anything like as highly as that. That they'd be a huge haul for a thief is no doubt true. But that they represent life or death for the Ospreys as a clan strikes me as totally untenable.'

'No doubt that puts them accurately in their place, metaphorically speaking. Just what or where their place is literally is one of our minor puzzles at the moment.'

'I wouldn't call it a minor puzzle at all,' Ringwood interposed. 'That Lord Osprey was killed by a crook who was after the things – and who may, or may not, have got away with them – is the best hypothesis we can work from at the moment. Or so it seems to me. I'm not so sure about Sir John here.' Ringwood was steadily gaining in confidence *vis-à-vis* the almost legendary John Appleby. 'He's made me rather interested in a fellow called Trumfitt, who wouldn't be much on the spot where antique coins are concerned.'

'Certainly not, if it's the Trumfitt I know.' Mr Brackley was amused. 'It's the rip-roaring giant at the pub?'

'That's the man,' Appleby said. 'Not, one imagines, exactly spot-on in the world of numismatics. Just what do you know about him?'

'That he has a picturesque local history as a man of violence. Much of it may be purely legendary, and promoted by himself as attractive to his clientele. But he has in fact been in trouble once or twice with the beaks, and keeps good order in his pub as a result. He can't find that difficult, being what one may call one of nature's chuckers-out. Rather lost, I'd say, in our fairly orderly community. He'd make a very good career as a bouncer at some Soho dive.' Mr Brackley was clearly proud of his command of a demotic English idiom here. 'In the army at one time, I've been told, but came out in a hurry. Himself bounced, it may have been.'

'Possessed of considerable cunning as well?'

'That I can't say, but it's likely enough. Just how has he come into your picture, Sir John?'

'Mr Ringwood here has dropped into The Osprey Arms. And Trumfitt himself dropped in on us here at Clusters only an hour ago, accompanied by a wronged daughter called Avice. The latest wrong suffered by the lady had been at the hands of the late Lord Osprey.'

'Indeed!' The vicar was at once serious. 'Tell me about it, please.'

So Appleby gave an account of the incident, more or less repeating what he had told Ringwood.

'And it is just conceivable,' he concluded, 'that the fellow's turning up on us was a bluff, and that he had the best of reasons for knowing that Lord Osprey was already dead.'

'Tricky,' Mr Brackley said.

'Have you any reason to feel that, so far as Avice and the dead man are concerned, there is some substance in the story?'

'I've never set eyes on this Avice Trumfitt.'

200

The vicar paused, as if aware that this was scarcely a communicative reply. And then he spoke again. 'No,' he said. 'There's nothing more that I can say. A parish priest, Sir John, is obliged to listen to a good deal of gossip. But, if he isn't to lose the confidence of his flock, he is forced to treat some of it as if it came to him in the confessional. You must excuse me, I am afraid.'

This, although falling short of the portentous, had to be final for the moment, and Appleby accompanied the vicar in silence into open air. Pausing in the portico, they had a glimpse of a man spraying with a hose the Osprey Rolls-Royce. The vicar's bicycle, which had the appearance of having seen much service, was perched beside a huge flight of steps.

'How are the bats?' Appleby asked, seeking a neutral topic.

'*Distinguo,* Sir John. The clerkly bats in my belfry are, I am glad to say, still undisturbed. Not so, it would appear, with the lay bats – and they are far more numerous – at the home farm. The boys over there, it seems, have been indulging in a bat *battue.*'

'Dear me! I've taken part, I'm afraid, in a pigeon *battue.* That is barbarous but at least rational, since flocks of pigeons can devastate a crop. But slaughtering bats wholesale seems utterly gratuitous.'

'Happily it has not been wholly effective. The majority of the lay bats, in fact, would seem to have survived. But if I were one of them, I would justly feel enraged.' This had the air of being offered as a valedictory remark, and the vicar was already astride his bicycle. He appeared, however, to think better of pushing off, and paused with the tips of both feet on the ground. 'I hope,' he said, 'that your colleague is right about that crook being after the wretched coins, and killing poor Osprey when surprised by him, and so on. I don't quite like the Trumfitt theory, if only because it seems likely to trail a certain amount of dirty linen behind it. But – and much more strongly – I dislike the possibility of its having been an inside job, if that's the term. A family affair, I mean.'

'Quite so, Mr Brackley. But, at the moment at least, the weight of the evidence is dead against anything of the sort. Osprey's wife and son and brother-in-law, together with the entire little bunch of guests, were decidedly in the wrong place when the curtain went up on the mystery. Oddly so, in a way, and almost as if there were something stagy and contrived about it. Almost like what I believe is called a sealed-room affair – in which, of course, the room turns out not to have been sealed after all.' For a moment Appleby paused, frowning over this. 'I've an odd feeling that something may yet turn up in that quarter. But, meanwhile, whatever is the opposite of an inside job must make all the running. As for Trumfitt, I'm afraid he offers, so to speak, the worst of both worlds. He's outside, all right, but with what you call dirty linen thick on him.'

'Meaning that, in burying Oliver Osprey, we'd be standing at the graveside of an elderly ravisher, were Trumfitt's yarn to prove to have any truth in it. It's a disagreeable thought.' The vicar shook his head over this, and for a moment seemed lost in thought. 'Do you know?' he said suddenly. 'What you want, Sir John, is a few mysterious strangers lurking in the neighbourhood. And it occurs to me that I can provide at least one of them. Do you know The Three Feathers in Great Clusters?'

'My wife and I have dined there once or twice. Quite unusually good food, but uncommonly expensive. Why do you ask?'

'It's run by a man called Fothergill, a bit of a scholar turned restaurateur. I knew him at

Balliol long ago, and have a word with him every now and then. In the street, that's to say. If I were seen going into the place my bank manager would have a fit. But I ran into Fothergill a couple of days ago, and he told me about an American – as he apparently is – of the name of Rackstraw. An etymologist would maintain that he must be a stingy fellow, but in fact he seems to be both opulent and regardless. He turned up at The Three Feathers in a Cadillac, booked himself a little suite of rooms, and appears to have done nothing much since. A waiter who takes him in drinks occasionally says he spends a good deal of time poring over a stamp album.'

'A stamp album.'

'Yes, a stamp album – which does now suddenly strike me as what you might call a near miss. What do you think?'

'Stamps are on a distinctly lower intellectual plane than coins. One associates them with King George V – a blameless monarch, but not exactly a master mind. But there's certainly a whiff of mystery about your Rackstraw, vicar. I'll have it looked into.' Appleby spoke with rather more conviction than he in fact felt. To be thus handed a mysterious stranger on, as it were, a plate, might have made him positively suspicious of an informant less transparently honest than Mr Brackley. 'And if any further problematical persons come within your purview,' he added, 'do let me know – or let Ringwood know – at once.'

'And, meanwhile, I'll take myself off.' As he said this, Mr Brackley put a foot on a pedal, maintained the balance of his machine by a deft waggle of the front wheel, and departed down the causeway. But an odd moment succeeded. A large and fast-moving car appeared, making for Clusters. Mr Brackley, momentarily glancing backwards, accorded Appleby what appeared to be intended as an informative sort of wave. In doing this, he swerved slightly, and this alarmed the driver of the Cadillac (as it proved to be). So the car swerved too, and for a moment it seemed possible that each was going to land in the moat. But this misadventure was avoided by both parties, and the vicar of Little Clusters disappeared behind a light cloud of dust.

'May I ask whether I have the honour of speaking to Lord Osprey?'

The man driving the Cadillac spoke with what Victorian novelists are fond of calling a 'twang', and so was undoubtedly as American as was his car. Here, in fact, was Mr Rackstraw. It took Appleby a moment to digest the oddity of this.

'I'm afraid not,' he then said. 'My name is Appleby.'

'He wouldn't have been the cycler?'

'No. That was the local vicar. A Mr Brackley.'

'The Reverend Brackley.' Mr Rackstraw, who appeared to have a tidy mind, might have dropped this information into an appropriate pigeonhole. 'I'm visiting with Lord Osprey,' he said, 'but I haven't made a date with him. Would he be at home, Mr Appleby?'

'Sir John Appleby.' This was a very English politeness, being designed to save Mr Rackstraw from any mild solecism in company later. 'Which Lord Osprey are you meaning to call on?'

'Which? There's can't be two Lord Osprey's, can there?' Mr Rackstraw looked at Appleby with some suspicion. 'Or can there? I'm not all that acquainted with such matters, Sir John.' Mr Rackstraw aware that he had got this form of address exactly right, eyed Clusters with a confident gaze. 'But there might be a dozen of them,' he said, 'and they'd still have quite a home.'

'I'm sorry – and I have to explain. Of course there is only one Lord Osprey at a time. But a Lord Osprey has just died, and his son – a young man called Adrian Osprey, who is actually in Clusters now – immediately succeeds to the title.'

'I see – and I'd better quit, I guess. The young man won't be feeling like doing business.'

'I think you are quite right there, sir. As a matter of fact, we have every reason to believe that his father has been murdered.'

'Murdered!'

'Just that. And perhaps I ought to say that I have myself some connection with the police who are investigating.'

'The young man will inherit everything?' Mr Rackstraw, although he had been given astounding news, clearly had a point and was resolved to stick to it.

'"Everything" is rather a comprehensive expression, is it not? I'm afraid I can't tell you.'

'It's the coins. The Osprey Collection. I'd corresponded with the lord, and intended to make an offer for it. But not, of course, sight unseen.'

'Of course not.' Appleby, although aware of having tumbled into a situation of extreme oddity, managed to remain matter of fact. 'I take it, sir, that you are yourself a determined collector of such things?'

Mr Rackstraw, who had got out of his car, was surveying the moat with disfavour.

'Messy,' he said. 'Not sanitary. But you're dead right about me. I collect in one field and another. But not without mastering the ground, Sir John. This Osprey Collection, now. I've had their catalogue, and I've been working on it in my apartment hotel in Great Clusters. A good class of book, and well illustrated. So I'd know at once if Lord Osprey – if *young* Lord Osprey, as it now is – were to be holding anything back. Yes, *sir.*'

This – Appleby thought – explained that waiter's impression of a stamp collection. But there seemed to be rather more about Mr Rackstraw that required explanation. Almost, he seemed a little too good to be true.

'This,' he asked suddenly and sharply, 'is the first time you've been out here?'

'At Clusters? It sure is. I do my homework thoroughly, as you might say.' Mr Rackstraw was clearly proud of his command of this expression.

'That car – did you bring it from America with you?'

'No, sir. They hired it me in London. One gets used to a thing. Lord Osprey, now – he would have been used to a Rolls?'

'I believe he was.'

'Thoroughbred little affairs. A look of class all over them.' Mr Rackstraw said this handsomely. 'But rather a lot of them around. In London you see queues of them.'

For Mr Rackstraw, Appleby reflected, 'London' probably meant the environs of the Connaught Hotel. But now the visitor had shaken hands and was climbing back into his hired car.

'Do I have to reverse?' he asked.

'By no means.' Appleby almost felt he had to vindicate the consequence of Clusters before this transatlantic visitor. 'Drive straight on. There's a courtyard in which you can turn easily enough.'

19

Following the Cadillac on foot, Appleby made several pauses to stare thoughtfully out over the moat. He recalled Ringwood as saying something to the effect that his men might have to end up by dredging it. The idea seemed an absurdity, and Ringwood had, of course, offered it as just that. The Osprey affair didn't run – as so many police hunts seemed to run nowadays – to a missing person and possibly a corpse. Nobody was missing – but what was missing was a collection of coins. No sooner had Appleby remembered this obvious fact than he found himself to have conjured up a distinctly odd visual image. It was of the late Lord Osprey suddenly at bay in his library, with the Osprey Collection in some obscure fashion under his hand, and an armed thief in front of him. With a speed and dexterity not in the least within Appleby's recollection or knowledge of Osprey as possessing, the collection's proprietor had wrenched open that French window and hurled his treasure into the darkness outside. It went down with a dull splash into the moat, and was thus safe from the unknown predator. Unknown, that was to say, to Appleby; he had to confess that he hadn't a clue as to whom it might have been; nobody knew except Lord Osprey himself; and Lord Osprey was very swiftly dead and silenced.

Appleby broke off from this bizarre fantasy to give a perfunctory wave to Mr Rackstraw, who had now succeeded in turning his car, and was presumably on his way back to what he had called his apartment hotel. But the renewed sight of Rackstraw put another idea in Appleby's head – not, this time, of a cinematic sort, but simply as a concept already formed in the mind. The Osprey Collection was proving uncommonly elusive – so did it any longer exist as entitled to be *called* the Osprey Collection in the full sense? Osprey, if the little man Purvis was to be believed, had been hard up and looking round for money on a substantial scale. Rackstraw had perhaps got wind of the fact. Had he not, indeed, claimed to have been in correspondence with Lord Osprey? Conceivably another would-be purchaser had got ahead of him, and a deal had been done. All this made a perfectly coherent theory. The bird, so to speak, had already flown. With the Osprey Collection the sudden and violent death of Lord Osprey had nothing to do. In thinking up that notion of the collection's being beneath the muddy waters of the moat, Appleby had simply been barking up the wrong tree. The Case of the Barking Dog. The Osprey affair – at least up to the present moment – deserved, perhaps, to be called just that.

To a slightly operatic effect, as if to deliver himself of a resounding solo, Detective-Inspector Ringwood was standing in the middle of the marble-clad hall.

'Who might that have been?' he asked with unaccustomed brusquerie. The afternoon was advancing, and little progress being made. Although not an edgy man, Ring-wood was almost irritable.

'An enormously affluent American called Rackstraw. He wanted to buy those blasted coins. I explained to him that a deal wasn't really practicable at the moment, and that a new Lord Osprey must be given time to play himself in.'

'You might have invited him to come in and look for the blessed things.' Ringwood was now gloomy. 'We need all the help we can get. Incidentally, that key's no good.'

'The key to the mystery, we were calling it. Just how has it failed us?'

'My sergeant has been round every door on the ground floor of the house. There isn't one that hasn't got a key in it already. And always on the outside. The idea would be to make burglary more difficult that way. But I doubt whether anybody bothered to go round on such a locking-up chore every night.'

'Bagot might know.' Appleby paused on this familiar and not particularly useful thought. 'Did the sergeant take out every one, and try the one we found in its place?'

'Certainly he did.'

'I still think the key may be important, Ringwood. Partly because of just where we found it, and partly because I feel the coins lived somewhere here on the ground floor. I was right in thinking that Clusters doesn't run to lifts or elevators, was I not?'

'Quite right. There used to be a couple of hoists from the old kitchens. But the whole place was modernized some time back, and all the offices, as they say, transferred to this floor. Troglodytes in short supply on the market, I suppose.'

'That would be it, no doubt.' Appleby betrayed no surprise at this learned flight on Ringwood's part. 'Where is the key now?'

'Here in my pocket.'

'Let me have it – would you?'

So Appleby was given the key, and dropped it into his own pocket.

'A memento,' Ringwood said a shade morosely, 'of a case that didn't run too smoothly.'

'*Nil desperandum*, Ringwood. And – do you know? – I have an odd feeling that has once or twice come to me before. Rather long ago, I'm afraid. It's a feeling of really knowing something that I just haven't managed to put salt on the tail of. A something that quite infuriatingly eludes me for the moment. But it's my guess that it will bob up again. As with the poet, you know. From hiding-places ten years deep.'

Ringwood received these remarks unfavourably.

'I can't see,' he said, 'that this nasty business has much to do with poetry.'

'Well, no. And ten years is a bit steep. Ten days might be nearer the mark.' Appleby frowned. 'Ringwood,' he asked, 'what the devil was I doing ten days ago?'

'Would that have been when you were

lunching here, Sir John?'

'Great heavens, man! You're right.'

But now there came a diversion. Marcus Broadwater had appeared. He came to a halt with an air of slightly ironic diffidence.

'Am I interrupting a conference?' he asked.

'If we are engaged in that way,' Appleby said, 'we'll be glad to have you join us.'

'You are very good. As a matter of fact, I was thinking of seeking you out. Some of our friends are getting impatient again. They want to know when they can leave.'

'That's very natural. I suppose Quickfall and the Wimpoles and Purvises will be bound for London. And I'd say, at a venture, that they will be able to catch the last evening train.'

If this reply surprised Broadwater (and it certainly surprised Ringwood) he gave no sign of the fact.

'Excellent!' he said. 'I'll give them the good news. If, of course, there *is* such a train. Surely they get scarcer and scarcer. Are you a reader of Trollope, Sir John? I've noticed in his novels that there always is a train, and his people keep on catching it. And they're scarcely more than the second generation of train travellers, are they not? *Autres temps, autres moeurs.* It's not so long ago that, visiting Clusters, I'd have had a man with me. And in our present distressing exigency, he'd have been in my room, hard at work sewing a mourning band on the sleeve of one of my jackets. And when I was an undergraduate and our last king died, we were told to go out and buy black ties, and wear them until after the funeral. All that's a thing of the past, and vanished with the horrific slaughters of the last war. Death has become cheapened – and, as a consequence, life as well. Wouldn't you say, Mr Ringwood?'

Ringwood scarcely concealed his disapproval of this fluent patter.

'There's a train from Great Clusters at eight forty-two,' he said.

'That should suit our friends very well – and I rather think I'll catch it myself. I wonder whether anyone any longer simply orders himself a special train? It still wasn't uncommon at the turn of the century – although always, I imagine, on the expensive side.' Broadwater paused on this. 'Or shall I stick to my plan of an evening's fishing?' he said. 'All things considered, I think I will.'

'Whether you do the one thing or the

other,' Appleby said a shade grimly, 'I wonder whether you'd answer a question or two first. Have you ever heard of a man called Rackstraw?'

'What an extraordinary name! Definitely not. Does he come into our present picture?'

'He's a wealthy American, and was here not half an hour ago. He wants to buy the Osprey Collection.'

'How excessively odd! The coins do keep on turning up on us, do they not?'

'They do, indeed. And I have at least your word for it, Mr Broadwater, that they do exist. But you and I have talked about their excessive elusiveness only a short time ago. I'd much like to see them, I have to admit. By the way, can you tell me anything about this?' Appleby's hand had gone to a pocket, and now it was extended to Broadwater with the mysterious key on its palm.

'It's a key,' Broadwater said calmly. 'What of it?'

'What, indeed?'

'Just where does it come from, Sir John?'

'From nowhere, seemingly. It's not like the key of a drawer or strong-box, but rather of an honest-to-God door. Wouldn't you say? And rather distinguished in its way. But it could be duplicated by a locksmith, I suppose, readily enough. So far as the business part goes, that is.'

'May I ask how you came by it, Sir John?'

'We found it in the library,' Appleby said – and now he was speaking rather casually. 'I have a notion that the Osprey Collection may lie, so to speak, on the other side of it. But I believe I've failed to convince Mr Ringwood here, so let me pass to something else. It's about that fellow Trumfitt. I gather you spend a good deal of time at Clusters, so perhaps you know something about him. Has he, would you say, a bit of a reputation for violence?'

'I've no idea.' Broadwater now sounded slightly impatient. 'I suppose he gave something of that impression when he favoured us with that visit a little time ago. I've seen him, when I took a walk near his pub, hard at work drowning some kittens. But that's a common enough rural pursuit. As for the yarn about his daughter, I suspect he was trumping up a good deal out of very little.'

'But out of something, nevertheless?'

'My dear Sir John, I am not prepared to discuss my late brother-in-law's character. It would be a most unseemly thing.'

'Even if it were to help to elucidate his murder?'

'Even then. It is something that close relatives ought never to be catechised about.'

And having delivered himself of this high-minded remark, Broadwater gave a curt nod and walked away. It was with evident displeasure that Detective-Inspector Ringwood watched him go.

'I can't make that fellow out at all, Sir John,' he said. 'Accosts you, one might say, with a mass of fluent jabber – and when that dries up, he just walks out on you. A regular play-acting type.'

'Perfectly true, Ringwood. I had it all from him when on my way here this morning. An actor in search of a role, you might say. And perhaps that is a role in itself.'

Ringwood received this cryptic remark in silence, as if its logic required thought.

'Histrionic,' he then said. 'That's the word for him. But it applies equally, if you ask me, to some of the rest of them. There's that high-up lawyer, for example.'

'Quickfall? I suppose that's true. But Quickfall is rather different. He has a real stage, and makes his living on it. Actors and barristers flock together. There's a London club that's pretty well full of them.'

'There's the bench and there's the bar, sir. But for a bit of real drama, you have to add the dock. And it's the dock we have to be thinking of.'

'You are right there, Ringwood. And if we're to get somebody into it – figuratively speaking – before this day is out, we must keep moving.'

'Are you really thinking, Sir John, that we can get this whole messy mystery tied up before nightfall?'

'Round about then, I'd rather hope. And we can begin by going back to your incident room. I think that's what you call it nowadays.'

'You'd be meaning the Music Saloon?'

'Just that. I've a notion it's the other place in which some key to this affair may lie.'

20

There was a constable on duty outside the Music Saloon, but the interior was untenanted except for a single policewoman brooding over a telephone on the platform. She was the same young person on whose good looks Appleby had commented to Ringwood earlier in the day. Ringwood, he felt, had disapproved, so perhaps some convention obtained in the matter. When Appleby had first found himself in the Metropolitan Police it had still been virtually a one-gender affair.

'What made you decide to pitch your tent here?' he asked Ringwood, glancing round the enormous chamber. 'It's impressive in its way, I suppose, and dates from a period in which conspicuous expenditure was still largely the perquisite of an aristocracy.'

'No doubt. And I chose it as the place seemingly least likely to inconvenience the household. It's clear that in the normal course of things nobody ever comes near it.'

'But even a single person needn't feel

exactly lonesome – not with all this proliferation of outsize looking-glasses. Dozens of you visible to yourself wherever you stand. Multiplying monotony in a wilderness of mirrors.' Appleby paused on this ingenious misquotation, which was, however, lost on his companion. 'I wonder how long it is? Promenade round it two or three times, and you'll have managed a healthy before-dinner walk.'

Having offered this idle remark, Appleby embarked on a perambulation that might have been suggested by it. And when he had been twice round the room, scanning the walls as he moved, he came to a halt.

'Yes,' he said. 'Yes, indeed. Parallax, Ringwood. Have you ever reflected on parallax?'

'Parallax?' Ringwood was displeased – and justifiably so. It is undeniable that John Appleby, when excited, is a little given to teasing remarks. 'It sounds like something you get from the chemist.'

'It's the apparent movement of one object in relation to another when the eye is moved. Think of looking out through the window of a railway-train as it hurtles along – hurtles your eye along. Everything seems to be scampering past everything else, with only the horizon in something near repose.

That's parallax. And it's the great enemy of illusionism in art – or in life, for that matter. Shift your stance only a little, and you know at once whether what's in front of you exists in three dimensions or only in two: whether it's an actual landscape, say, or simply a painting of one. What's in front of our noses now?'

'A half-open door, with a little lobby beyond it. And in the wall beyond that there's a second door, which is closed.'

'Move on a pace, Ringwood. Parallax is operating, remember. So the farther door ought to have begun to edge out of view, ought it not? Well, has it?'

'Of course it hasn't.' Ringwood, although now far from at sea, accepted good-humouredly this note of catechism. 'It hasn't because the whole thing is a silly fake. It's the blessed *trompe-l'œil*, as they call it. There's really hardly any lobby at all, and the farther door, together with the harp perched in front of it, is much nearer than it appears to be, and no more than paint on canvas.'

'I agree that there's hardly any real lobby there. But the second door is a real door, although the harp, indeed, is no more than pigment, skilfully applied. In fact, Ring-wood, the Clusters *trompe-l'œil* is a *trompe-*

l'œil trompe-l'œil.'

'Or a *trompe-l'œil* with knobs on.' Ringwood was rather pleased with this. 'And are you suggesting, Sir John…?'

'Of course I am. The door supposed to be no more than canvas has a keyhole, hasn't it?' For the second time in half an hour Appleby's hand went to a pocket. 'So here's our blessed key again,' he said. 'Try it, Ringwood.'

And Detective-Inspector Ringwood put the solid key in the keyhole of an equally solid door. He turned a solid door-knob, and the door swung open.

'The bloody coins!' he said.

Senior officers of police, when on duty, commonly refrain from improper language. But on this occasion, Appleby felt, Ringwood was decidedly to be excused.

'Almost certainly so,' he said. 'And there's what that chap Broadwater told me was like a trolley in a restaurant. That scarcely does the affair justice, would you say? Trundle it out, Ringwood. It doesn't look as if it trundled, but I'll be surprised if it fails to.'

Ringwood did as he was told – and without great effort, although the entire Osprey Collection was under his hand.

'Moves like a high-class kid's pram,' he said. 'And all those shallow drawers! I'll bet they move like a dream. If Louis Quatorze or somebody of that sort had ordered a filing cabinet, this is what would have been respectfully delivered to him. Worth a mint of money in itself, I'd say. You can imagine it in one of those grand auctioneer's catalogues.'

'Quite so. Beautifully sprung, and with its wheels concealed behind exquisite joinery. A veritable Cadillac of a filing cabinet. Mr Rackstraw himself would be impressed by it.' Appleby's enthusiasm was perhaps tinged with irony. 'One positively hesitates to explore further. But pull out one of those drawers, Ringwood.'

Ringwood did so.

'The coins, all right,' he said. 'Not all that impressive, this lot. Rather like old halfpennies and farthings. But each of them snug in a little velvet berth.'

'Try another one.'

The second drawer opened to reveal a blaze of gold. And for a few moments Appleby and Ringwood gazed at one another, much as a couple of conquistadors might have done if suddenly confronted with some treasure of the Incas.

'We can't keep this to ourselves,' Appleby said abruptly. 'Under present circumstances, the whole caboodle ought to be lodged in the strong-room of a bank. And the first thing to do is to call in Lord Osprey.'

'Lord Osprey, Sir John?' Ringwood spoke rather as if supposing that Appleby was proposing to summon up the dead.

'The *new* Lord Osprey, Ringwood. Young Adrian. Until the family lawyers do their stuff, it must be presumed that he is the owner of the things.'

'No doubt you are right, sir. Shall I go and hunt him out?'

'I think better not. Give a hail to that young woman up on the platform. She's already goggling at us. Nobody should be left alone with this eminently pocketable stuff until Adrian has been brought in on it. If valuable coins turn out to be missing from it, heaven knows what a chap like our friend Quickfall might get up to asking about in open court. But he'd scarcely get round to suggesting sudden criminal collusion between the two of us.'

'I see what you mean.' Ringwood was already beckoning to the young policewoman. He was clearly impressed, even if slightly shocked by this swift – if no doubt routine –

professional prudence. 'What about Broad-water – if he hasn't gone off to his fishing again? He's a numismatist, I gather, and has actually worked on the stuff.'

'So he has – but I don't think we need trouble him at present, all the same. Get your girl to say, however, that we suggest Lord Osprey bring Miss Wimpole along with him. She's a numismatist too, and shaping to be a good deal involved with this place.'

'How would that be, Sir John?'

'As the next Lady Osprey, Ringwood. It's as plain as a pikestaff. Not that either of them is as yet quite aware of the fact.' And John Appleby (who had a weakness for being pleased with his own sagacity) laughed softly. 'It's the only reasonably cheerful thing,' he added, 'that's likely to emerge from this mess.'

So presently Adrian and Honoria appeared, and Appleby explained what he shamelessly called Mr Ringwood's discovery.

'Did you know of the existence of this hiding-place?' he asked the young man.

'I hadn't a clue. But I did know that my father was rather given to tucking small sums of money oddly away. Five-pound notes in matchboxes. That sort of thing.'

'Adrian,' Honoria said, 'has the misfortune of being the son of a pathological miser. As a consequence, he's no doubt likely to turn into a spendthrift.'

'Shut up, Honoria. Your sense of humour would disgrace a kindergarten.'

'An old folk's home, you ought to say. I'm a great deal older than you are, young man.'

'Three years and four weeks,' Adrian answered with surprising speed. And at this Appleby gave Ringwood a swift and almost imperceptible nod. Here, it seemed to say, was incontrovertible evidence of his late assertion.

'The first thing to insist on the importance of,' Appleby said to Adrian, 'is getting this very valuable collection of coins into a place of greater security than that afforded by Clusters' celebrated, if not fully understood, *trompe-l'œil* affair. It was an eccentric choice, to say the least, on your father's part. But another matter is urgent, too, and I hope Miss Wimpole will be good enough to help us with it. What is the present state of the Osprey Collection? Is everything that should be there, *there?* What is obviously a copy of the fairly recently published catalogue is lying on the top of the cabinet, or whatever it is to be called. Perhaps that may be useful.'

Honoria turned to Adrian.

'Shall I?' she asked.

'Yes, of course. Go ahead. Clusters is turning into a sort of *Treasure Island*. Pieces of eight, pieces of eight, pieces of eight!' Adrian was pretending to be Long John Silver's parrot. 'Eight what, Honoria?'

'*Reales*, Adrian. Spanish dollars. Sir John, here, has read about them in *Don Quixote*. I'll find you one to play with presently. If you'd lived in Rambang in the earlier eighteenth century, you could have bought a cow for two of them.'

'I'm glad I didn't.'

'Just be quiet, and let me get some sort of grip on the stuff.' Having said this – and having said it, by implication, both to Detective-Inspector Ringwood and Sir John Appleby – Honoria Wimpole studied the Osprey Collection for some time. The catalogue, she consulted only occasionally. But she pulled out every one of the little drawers in turn, surveyed the contents with care, and every now and then picked out a single coin and scrutinized it carefully. Finally, and when she had closed the last of the drawers, she sat back in silence for several minutes, clearly putting in order what she could most usefully say.

'To begin with,' she then began, 'I ought perhaps to explain that the collection is basically what used to be thought of as a gentleman's cabinet, a polite accessory to a polite education. No particular emphasis; just a general assembly of coins, slanted on the whole to the classical field – which is, of course, quite enormous in itself. It's that sort of collection on a pretty grand scale. There is, however, the beginning of a sensible concentration on one important field or another – and in that we can perhaps see the influence of Adrian's Uncle Marcus. I could have told you all this without ever entering this room. And what I have now discovered, any qualified person could have discovered simply by looking at the collection with adequate care.'

Saying this, Honoria pulled out one of the drawers, and pointed to a small coin near the middle of it.

'Mr Ringwood,' she then said, 'will you just take a straight glance at this one, and tell us whose head is on it?'

Not without a shade of reluctance, Ringwood obeyed this behest.

'It's Edward VII,' he then said. 'And the coin must be something I don't think I've ever seen before. It's a half sovereign.'

'Exactly. And, according to the catalogue, it ought to be a gold coin of rather more antiquity: a stater of Demetrius Poliorcetes, King of Macedon, round about 250 BC.'

Ringwood being rendered momentarily speechless before this mystery, it fell to Appleby to say something.

'In other words, Miss Wimpole, the Osprey Collection has been – well, milked?'

'Just that – although nowhere else, so far as I've yet discovered, with quite that degree of impudence. It's a matter of a good many rare, and therefore very valuable, coins being removed, and there being set in their place other old coins of no particular rarity or value. An ignoramus simply wouldn't notice.' Having said this, Honoria Wimpole sat back abruptly, and when she spoke again, it was on quite a different note. 'So, in God's name,' she said, 'whatever do we do?'

'Ask Bagot. Bagot knows everything.'

This attempt, on Adrian's part, to import a certain lightness of air into the sudden crisis signally failed. Appleby, indeed, may scarcely have heard it. He was reflecting that he had himself called Lord Osprey an ignoramus – but that had been to Judith ten days before.

'So,' he asked, 'it might have been quite some time before Lord Osprey tumbled to the thing?'

And at this Honoria, although not normally at all a hesitant person, did hesitate.

'I suppose that is undeniably true,' she then said.

After this, there was a long silence. The young policewoman, back on her dais, had become ostentatiously absorbed in some clerkly activity. The counsels of princes, she may have felt, are not prudently to be overheard.

'It's beginning to come clear,' Ringwood eventually said, and looked doubtfully at Appleby.

But Appleby remained silent. He had suddenly seen himself as knowing something probably not known to anybody else, except conceivably to Lord Osprey's murderer. It was as if a voice had spoken from the dead. It was as if such a voice had spoken very briefly; had uttered, indeed, but a single word – a single word, however, of portentous effect.

Appleby's first impulse was to communicate his discovery – if discovery it was – to his companions there and then. He felt that he had almost a duty to do so. For if he himself happened to be murdered by a bullet from afar here and now, or even to suffer some lethal seizure as he sat, neither Ringwood nor anybody else was by any means certain to arrive at knowledge perhaps crucial to the elucidation of the Clusters mystery.

But *was* it knowledge? Or was it, on the contrary, a mere ingenious fantasy, prompted by the odd chime of a word? Appleby decided, for the time being at least, to hold his hand – or his tongue. It wasn't merely early days with the Osprey enigma; almost, it was early hours. A good deal had happened – or, rather, had been talked about – and it wasn't yet quite tea-time for the Ospreys and their guests. So the present talk might reasonably be carried a little further. Something might emerge from it. But caution was required. What to Ringwood was 'beginning to come clear' had best be kept under wraps for the moment.

'I rather gather,' he said to Honoria, 'that you were hoping that Lord Osprey might himself show you this collection either today or tomorrow. Had that happened, you could hardly have failed to make then the discovery you have made now. Is that right?'

'I suppose so.'

'Had that happened – had you, for example, noticed that half sovereign masquerading as something uttered by Demetrius Poliorcetes – would you have drawn Lord Osprey's attention to it?'

'Isn't that what is called a hypothetical question, Sir John?'

'No doubt it is, but I see no reason why you shouldn't answer it.'

'You know very well why I don't much care for it. It introduces the question of whether Lord Osprey himself hadn't been doing what you call the milking. If he had been selling off one or two very valuable coins in a quiet way, and artlessly dropping mediocre substitutes in their place, I might well have hesitated to pounce on the thing. It wouldn't have been exactly tactful. And as what I'd detected could only be called a childish or muddle-headed foible, with nothing of real deceit about it, my speaking up could quite fairly be considered as impertinent as well.'

'But, Miss Wimpole, consider the context in which we now have to consider all this. Lord Osprey has been murdered, and we have to do our best to decide whether or not the Osprey Collection has been some sort of motivating factor. That the coins have nothing to do with the case is a tenable view. The fellow who burst in on us so angrily at lunch-time will no doubt come into your head there. But he may well be totally irrelevant to our real concern, and both Mr Ringwood and I incline to the view that the coins are indeed central to the case. You have now inspected them at leisure, and have yourself raised the possibility that Lord Osprey had himself been quietly parting with some of the most valuable things and replacing them with coins of altogether inferior worth. Obviously it is a possibility. But are you inclined to view that state of the case as probable? That's what I'd like to get at.'

'Definitely not.' Honoria gave this reply without hesitation. 'And for two reasons. The first is simply that half sovereign. Substituting that for a coin of the third century BC was a freakish act that doesn't at all fit in with my conception of Lord Osprey's character. But my second reason is much more substantial. Lord Osprey definitely led me to feel that I was going to be shown his collection either today or tomorrow. And he knew perfectly well that my interest in it would be informed and professional.'

'So you are driven to suppose that he was

unaware of what had happened to his collection. If it had been happening slowly over a considerable period of time, could his ignorance – call it his numismatic innocence – have been such that he might not notice something amiss?'

'I think so. The substitutions, so far as I have spotted them during this brief rummage, are not startling at a mere glance. Where a coin of considerable antiquity has been abstracted, it is generally a coin of some antiquity – but of very little value today – that has been put in its place.'

'That half sovereign,' Ringwood interrupted. 'You can't say that of it?'

'No, indeed. It's almost like a joke. Or not so much a joke as a dare. A hostage given to fortune.'

'A what?' Adrian asked.

'Or somebody saying "Catch who catch can". I find it distinctly odd.'

'It's *all* distinctly odd,' Adrian complained. 'I can't get to the bottom of it, at all. I knew there were a lot of old coins my father was interested in, but not anything about all this hiding them away. It's the sort of thing misers do, all right. At Harrow they made me read a book about one. Silas somebody. It's by a woman.'

'Women do sometimes write books, Adrian.'

It seemed to Appleby that there was more of affection than mockery in this remark. But that was by the way. More important was his sense that the Osprey mystery was now moving. And Ringwood, he knew, had the same feeling. But Ringwood still saw a difficulty that Appleby didn't.

Because of that chime of a single word.

21

But Appleby had schooled himself to distrust hunches and flashes of inspiration. Often enough they had proved to be false lights leading either nowhere or into embarrassing situations which it had required a good deal of skill to get out of. Perhaps it might be so now. He was on the verge, as it were, of standing the entire Osprey affair on its head, and this on the strength of an odd association of ideas which would distinctly cut no ice in a court of law. He could almost hear the accents in which some criminal barrister like the fellow Quickfall might hold it up to ridicule before a judge and jury.

Before sharing his hazardous new perception even with Ringwood, it would be wise to find some sort of concrete evidence or, failing that, at least some concurring opinion. And here Appleby thought of Bagot. It seemed to be a general opinion at Clusters that Bagot should be consulted about this, or would know all about that. So Appleby decided to have another go at Bagot, and that on this occasion it should be a tête-à-tête affair, without the support of Ringwood. Bagot and Ringwood hadn't got along together too well.

This proved easy. Hard upon the conference with Honoria Wimpole the Detective-Inspector had been called away to the telephone to give some complicated instructions about matters unrelated to the Osprey enquiry. And it was a little after five o'clock; a tea-drinking in the drawing-room was drawing to a close; but this was without the attendance of Bagot, for whose superintendence it was too trivial an occasion. Bagot, in fact, was having tea served to him in his pantry by a nervous junior parlour maid, and Appleby found him there. Bagot was good enough to intimate to his underling that a cup should be provided for Sir John.

'It has occurred to me, Mr Bagot,' Appleby said, 'that you and I might usefully have another word together. Of a confidential character, you understand. There is the question, for instance, of Lord Osprey's nervous tone – I think that is the best expression – during the few days leading up to this terrible occasion. Would you, who are a keen observer, describe it as wholly normal?'

'A most interesting question, Sir John.' For some moments Bagot was silent, probably thinking of himself as making a weighty pause. 'To my mind, his lordship was disturbed. Or perturbed. I think that on the whole, perturbed might be the better word.'

'I see. Have you any notion of what he might have been perturbed about? Could it have been, for instance, a matter of money worries?'

'I think not. Financial embarrassments incline to exercise a depressing effect, do they not? And his lordship was not depressed. And now I have thought of a better word still. His lordship was jumpy.'

'Jumpy, was he?' Appleby found this sudden drop into vernacular expression on the ponderous Bagot's part worthy of note. 'Had you any feeling that he had to be handled carefully?'

'Indeed, yes. In some degree it is always a necessity, of course, in my profession. Employers of upper servants are in general a kittle crowd.'

'I suppose that to be true.' Appleby felt that a new Bagot was beginning to emerge. 'What would Lord Osprey be jumpy about?'

'Well, Sir John, there was that man – and his allegations. His lordship may have scented trouble there some time before the man's scandalous irruption today.'

'I see.' Appleby wondered whether he might venture to enquire if it was Bagot's belief that his late employer had valid cause to feel jumpy in what might be termed the general Avice region. But he decided to refrain. 'You felt you had to handle Lord Osprey carefully,' he said. 'Even, perhaps, to the point of occasional – well, equivocation?'

'Indeed, yes.' Bagot was quite unperturbed by this admission.

'Allow me to recur, Mr Bagot, to the incident in the library before dinner last night. It seems to me to call for careful analysis.'

'Does it indeed, Sir John?' Bagot seemed suddenly wary. 'I think I may say that I agree.' The wariness increased. 'In the sense, that is, that the whole shocking affair requires careful handling.'

'No doubt it does. But now, Mr Bagot, I want to confide in you. To confide in you and place a high degree of confidence in your judgement. Nothing has more impressed me at Clusters than the general – indeed, the universal – regard in which that is held.' This was perhaps to carry the buttering up technique rather far, and Appleby made no pause. 'I want to tell you of something which I have come to relate closely to the episode at the window.' At this Appleby thought he saw the butler's gaunt form stiffen slightly. And he hurried on. 'It will be within your recollection that my wife and I had the pleasure of lunching here about ten days ago. There was some talk about bats in the parish church, and Lord Osprey appeared to feel that Lady Osprey had not given adequate thought to the matter. He begged her to reflect. That was his word, uttered with his frequent odd emphasis. And he repeated it later. *Reflect.*'

'I think, Sir John, that we are getting on delicate ground.'

'Of course we are.' Appleby was suddenly brusque. 'Just keep on listening to me for a little. The word, and its derivatives, may be used in several senses. One may *reflect* on something. Or one may see oneself *reflected* in a mirror.'

'And if one is in a well-lit room, and one advances to a window when it is dusk outside' – Bagot paused with a full sense of drama on this – 'one sees what is in fact one's own reflection approaching one. It is idle, Sir John, to deny that we are on common ground here.'

'Lord Osprey is in what you have called a

"jumpy" condition. He makes to close those curtains, imagines he sees an intruder, closes them abruptly, and cries out that an intruder is there. Miss Minnychip, an impressionable woman, believes herself to have seen what Lord Osprey believes himself to have seen – and the episode is over. Or not quite, Mr Bagot. There remains your own part in it. And that might be viewed unsympathetically by anyone not cognisant of the excellence of your motive. Its devotion, as it may justly be termed.' Appleby had taken his fence boldly, and the ball (slightly to vary the metaphor) was now in Bagot's court. And Bagot responded with admirable candour.

'Everything you say is true, Sir John.'

'And you were the only person in the room, Mr Bagot, with sufficient intelligence instantly to see the plain fact of the matter. You then went through – and you will forgive me the expression – something of a charade. You felt that Lord Osprey's nervous balance was in jeopardy, and you had the chauffeur join you in hunting for somebody you knew didn't exist. I am obliged to say that your failing to explain the matter of the reflection there and then seems to me to have been an error of judgement – as has been your reluctance to come forward with the truth of the matter later. But your motive was admirable. I wholly commend it.' Appleby was silent for a moment after telling this monstrous fib. 'But, at the same time, I must point out what very serious consequences have followed.'

'Serious consequences, Sir John?'

'Circumstances have conspired to persuade us all that there really was an intruder, and that he returned later by the same route and murdered Lord Osprey. This, once accepted at least as a hypothesis, eliminated an entire group of people from our enquiry. Everybody, in fact, who was in the library at the time of the first appearance of our supposed murderer. Once admit that that appearance was a figment – mere trick of optics, one may say – and the entire field is wide open again.'

'I think it was that Trumfitt,' Bagot said obstinately. 'Killing a man that way just wasn't refined. None of the family, and none of the guests either, would have done it just so. We've heard tell, I believe, of Trumfitt drowning kittens, and that's not far from killing pigs. And it's one that would do that might slit a human throat the way his lordship was.' Bagot's conviction here was obviously sincere. The collapse of his elegant English witnessed to the fact.

'I must go and have a word with the Detective-Inspector,' Appleby said. 'And with some of the family and guests too. Nobody has departed yet, I take it?'

'Not to my knowledge, sir. But I detect a certain mood of impatience to be abroad.'

'Do you indeed, Mr Bagot? I'm not sure I don't feel that way inclined myself.'

'There is talk of the late train from Great Clusters. It presents us with a small difficulty. A huddled dinner is always an uncomfortable affair. The cook and I have conferred on the matter, and our inclination is towards a light collation at seven o'clock.'

'That will be the best thing, no doubt.' Appleby, who didn't feel that he had anything to contribute to this particular problem, had moved towards the door of Bagot's pantry.

'And Mr Broadwater has taken sandwiches.'

'The dickens he has!' Appleby had come to a halt. 'Do you mean he has gone off fishing again?'

'Yes, indeed, Sir John. Mr Broadwater's devotion to rod and line is notorious among us. And he asked me to fill his pocket-flask with cognac, saying something about the treacherous evening vapours.'

'They are to be guarded against, no doubt – as all treachery has to be. Neglect that, and you may walk straight into danger.'

In the corridor, Appleby encountered Miss Minnychip. She stopped him.

'My dear Sir John! Such a curious thing. My housekeeper has just rung up to tell me.'

'Has she, indeed?' Appleby reflected that at Clusters he was decidedly encountering the moneyed classes. Even this maiden lady, who so clearly regarded herself as living on a shoe-string, employed a housekeeper. 'I hope the message was an agreeable one.'

'I don't think it was of *practical* interest. But gratifying, all the same. It was about a Mr Rackstraw. I think that was the name, although it sounds rather an odd one. He had paid a call, but without writing ahead. Rather on the informal side, that. But one knows what American's are.'

'An American, is he – this Mr Rackstraw?' Appleby's small dissimulation here was automatic; irony in its strictest Socratic sense had long been habitual with him. 'Did he leave word of what his business was?'

'It appeared that he wants to buy my late

father's collection of coins. Just think of that! Dealing in such things is Mr Rackstraw's regular line of business, it appears. And he is touring the country in pursuit of it.'

'That is most interesting.' Rackstraw, Appleby judged, when approaching a really major prize such as the Osprey Collection, presumably found it advantageous to convey the impression of enormous independent wealth. 'Are you going to be tempted by him?'

'Certainly not. Upon my death, all my property is to go to a great nephew, a thoroughly reliable young man. I have suggested to him that he presents the Minnychip Collection to the University of Oxford, which he will no doubt do.'

'That is very proper, no doubt.' Appleby found himself hoping that the great-nephew, faced with this presumably unexpected windfall, would indeed prove to be reliable. 'There is much to be said for moderation in collections of one sort or another. It is the really whopping ones that tend to bring trouble.'

'I suppose that to be so.' Miss Minnychip appeared slightly perplexed. 'Whopping' was perhaps a vulgarism outside her vocabulary.

'How hardly shall they that have riches,' she said, 'enter into the kingdom of God. And the rich he hath sent empty away. I hope that nothing of the kind befalls dear Adrian, now that he has entered upon so large a patrimony. Happily, Honoria Wimpole is a thoroughly sensible girl.'

This last remark startled Appleby a good deal, since he had believed himself alone in spotting which way the wind was blowing in that quarter.

'And I hope, Sir John, that this horrible murder is about to be cleared up.' Miss Minnychip had returned to practical matters. 'People are beginning to wonder about that last train. I myself simply drove over to Clusters, and have no problem. One knows, of course, what dreadful things can happen to motorists nowadays. But my journey, happily, is very short.'

'I am sure it will be entirely uneventful, Miss Minnychip. As for the mystery of Lord Osprey's death, it is now going to be cleared up in no time at all. There is nothing complicated about it.'

And with this drastic assessment of a day's work, Appleby took leave of Miss Minnychip, and went on his way to find Detective-Inspector Ringwood.

But first he found himself having to converse with Rupert Quickfall. The barrister was standing in a relaxed attitude, hands in pockets, before one of the two enormous windows flanking the main entrance to Clusters. He seemed to be eyeing with some displeasure the view thus afforded of the causeway with the moat on either side of it.

'Ah!' he said. 'Appleby. A bit of a mess, isn't it?'

'Well, not really, Quickfall. I rather think it's beginning to clear up a little.'

'Oh, *that!* I didn't mean the mystery of our host's nasty end. I meant merely its physical setting: this ridiculous agglomeration they call Clusters. Actually, it isn't a bad name for it, if it comes to that. A cluster of disparate architectural styles owning no kinship each with another. Walk around, and you don't know within half-a-dozen centuries just where you're perambulating. Naturally, nothing can be done about it now. But at least our deceased friend could have got rid of his absurd moat. Drained it, and filled it in, and brought his park right up to his windows as advocated long ago by dear old Capability Brown.'

'No doubt.' Appleby found this topic

singularly uninteresting, and had no inclination to disguise the fact.

'Dreary prospect,' Quickfall said, nodding towards the window. 'Tiresome time of year – and hour. Dusk beginning to gather already, but in an indecisive sort of way. A few bats around, and presently there will be a good many more. Did I hear you say the murder is due to solve itself soon?'

'It won't exactly do that. Not without a bit of a shove, you know. But there can be little doubt, to my mind, about the identity of the perpetrator.'

'Evidence?'

'That's rather a different matter. Just how things fell out as they did is, so far, distinctly to seek.'

'Not an unfamiliar state of the case, my dear Appleby. If you were a barrister, and had been in practice as long as I have, you'd know that the streets are crowded by men and women known with complete assurance to be homicides, but in whose particular case there just hadn't been anything like adequate evidence to take into court.'

'You wouldn't utter that bland exaggeration before a judge of the High Court on his bench, Quickfall. But I'd agree that there's a modicum of truth in it. And I'd

suppose, by the way, that I've been a policeman for a good deal longer than you have
been a barrister. And there's nobody that
knows better than a policeman does that a
case has to be all sewn-up and tidy before
you arrive in court with it.'

'You'll scarcely manage that by today's
bed-time, will you?'

'I rather think that this excellent man
Ringwood will decide to take a chance, and
have somebody locked up by midnight. If he
asks my advice, I'll do my best to give it
faithfully.'

Having thus formally resurrected what
can only be called a pious fiction, Appleby
gave a nod to the barrister, and went on his
way. He found Ringwood in the Music
Saloon.

22

'So that may have been it,' Ringwood said with some reluctance when Appleby had expounded to him as an indubitable fact the non-existence of the previous night's pre-prandial prowler. 'It's a common enough experience: a window turning into a shadowy sort of mirror under those conditions. But if, as we are told, Lord Osprey was in the habit of closing those library curtains himself at some evening hour, he must have been perfectly familiar with the phenomenon. Of course I admire, Sir John, the way your mind jumped to it from the word "reflect". But I remain a little uneasy about the thing. Why, since it must have been a regular action with him, should Lord Osprey have gone so astray on this occasion? I don't quite see it, sir.'

'He was jumpy, Ringwood. That's Bagot's word. Osprey was apprehensive that something was coming to him.'

'A thief after the coins, you mean?'

'I mean nothing of the sort. I mean Trumfitt.'

'But it was only when you were having lunch today…'

'It was only then that Trumfitt went public, as it may be put. But he may well have been threatening Lord Osprey privately for some time. And Osprey was jumpy probably because he had a bad conscience about Trumfitt's daughter.'

'Miss Minnychip, now…'

'Miss Minnychip yelped because Osprey had yelped. And she believes she had glimpsed what Osprey believed he had glimpsed. Bagot is a far sounder witness than Miss Minnychip.'

'Perfectly true,' Ringwood said candidly. He thought for a moment. 'That boat,' he said. 'It had been out on the water, all right. We both know that.'

'The boat, I admit, remains to be explained. And when it is, I think we'll have arrived at the heart of the matter.' Appleby paused, glancing with some caution at his colleague. 'But – to be frank about it – we believe we've got there already, do we not?'

'I believe so.' Ringwood seemed encouraged to speak out. 'Once we've got rid of Trumfitt, and got rid of the intruder who wasn't there, what we are left with is what you might call a family job.'

'Not quite that, Ringwood. There's Lady Wimpole, for instance – and Miss Minnychip and Mrs Purvis and Rupert Quickfall. Several others, too, who can't be described as family. Call it an inside job.'

Ringwood considered this.

'Hadn't we both better speak out, Sir John?' he then asked.

'Very well. Lord Osprey was killed by his brother-in-law, and you and I are now equally convinced of the fact.'

'Just that. But what's our evidence? And what do we not yet know that we ought to know, if the thing is to be brought home to the man?'

Appleby had accorded a brief nod to each of these questions.

'We know for a start,' he said, 'that somebody learned in numismatics has been pilfering from the Osprey Collection, substituting nearly worthless coins for very valuable ones. This may, or may not, have been achieved actually in Lord Osprey's presence. He turns out to have known astonishingly little about coins himself, so nothing but a little dexterity would be required to achieve the thefts. So Broadwater may, or may not, have known where the coins were kept. He may, or may not, have contrived both to know about the *trompe-l'œil* affair and to have achieved his own means of gaining access to it. We know – that is, we can clearly see – that there was a kind of flaunting impudence about the enterprise. It could only pass undetected for so long as Lord Osprey allowed no expert other than Broadwater himself to make any sustained scrutiny of that remarkable cabinet and its contents.'

'Miss Wimpole!' Ringwood said. 'It had become clear that within a couple of days Lord Osprey would have succumbed to that young woman's determined assault on the things.'

'You can put it that way, if you like. And remember that Lord Osprey was apparently feeling hard-up, and that the seemingly very wealthy – but also knowledgeable – Mr Rackstraw had been in correspondence with him. Broadwater may well have had wind of that. It all adds up, as they say – at least in the way of motive. But just what *happened?* At this present moment, Ringwood, we have nothing but guesswork to put before a judge and jury.'

'We do have a corpse, Sir John. And a weapon snatched from that affair on the wall. And there's the boat–' Ringwood broke off abruptly. 'Come to think of it,' he said, 'that damned boat is uncommonly inconvenient. For the case we're trying to build up, that's to say.'

'And just there, Broadwater was, so to speak, ahead of us. He'd killed his brother-in-law – and what the devil was he to do? He remembered the evening's fuss about an intruder who must have crossed the moat; he remembered about the little skiff in its shed; and he promptly saw in those things the means of laying a species of false trail. He slipped out of the house and across the moat by the causeway; made his way to the little boat-shed; launched the skiff and paddled it around sufficiently to get it thoroughly wet; he then berthed it and made his way back to the library. What had he achieved? A very broad hint to us that the killing of Lord Osprey had not been an inside job.'

The Detective-Inspector's response to this was to look rather glum.

'Sir John,' he asked at length, 'do you think that if we searched Broadwater's rooms here at Clusters now, we might come on some of those stolen coins?'

'No, Ringwood, I do not. Broadwater isn't a Whitechapel thicky, you know. He's a clever, if slightly crazy, man – a Cambridge don, and all that.'

'I think that, in a way, we've run ahead of ourselves, sir. We've started from a confront-ation of these two men, round about midnight or in the small hours. Just how did that come about? We know that Lord Osprey is in his pyjamas and dressing-gown, and we take a guess that that crucial key is in his pocket. Everybody else in Clusters is presumably asleep. Why this extraordinary meeting? What is it supposed to be about?'

'Indeed, why and what,' Appleby said. 'These questions are the nub of the matter. And until we can answer them, at least after some plausible fashion, we can't act – can we? When Broadwater returns from his fishing, it would be imprudent to have him taken away in a van.'

At this point the colloquy in the Music Saloon was interrupted by Bagot, who entered carrying a tray on which stood a decanter and two glasses.

'A glass of sherry, gentlemen,' Bagot said solemnly.

'It's a little on the early side, isn't it?' Appleby had glanced at his watch.

'I may remind you, Sir John, of the

advanced hour for the light collation.'

'But of course. And I am sure you always time these matters perfectly.' Appleby poured a glass of sherry, and handed it to Ringwood. He then helped himself. 'Just how is the house-party going to disband?' he asked.

'Miss Minnychip, who came over to Clusters in her car, will drive herself home. Miss Minnychip is a most independent lady. Having, as she has, only a small household may well have inclined her that way.'

At this, Ringwood, although sipping his sherry, might have been heard to utter a faint snort. It indicated, perhaps, mounting disapproval of Clusters in general, and dissent from the notion that driving a car over two or three miles of quiet country road testified to any great independence of character.

'And Robinson, Lord Osprey's chauffeur,' Bagot continued with dignity, 'will convey the rest of the party – Lady Wimpole and her daughter, Mr Quickfall, and Mr and Mrs Purvis – to the railway station in the Rolls.' Bagot, having produced these names in their correct order, bowed, and turned to withdraw.

'Just a moment.' Appleby glanced at his

colleague. 'Mr Ringwood,' he said. 'I think we might put our current problem to Mr Bagot – who is so thoroughly knowledgeable a man.'

To this Ringwood responded merely with a slight nod – thereby indicating that he deferred only to Sir John Appleby's seniority, and that no such irregular proposal would have come into his own head.

'It's like this, Mr Bagot,' Appleby then said. 'We have Lord Osprey in his pyjamas and dressing-gown, in the library round about midnight or the small hours, and there meeting or encountering an unknown person who appears to have lost little time in murdering him. Since making your formal statement to the Detective-Inspector this morning, has any further notion come to you as to how this situation or confrontation may have been occasioned?'

'In measure, yes, Sir John. It is not to be denied that *l'esprit de l'escalier* has been in operation.' Bagot paused on this impressive (if not strikingly appropriate) display of erudition. 'It has come to me as possibly relevant that Lord Osprey was a little given to nocturnal perambulation.'

'Do you mean that he was a sleep-walker – that sort of thing?'

'Not at all, Sir John.' Bagot appeared to find this possibility mildly shocking. 'I merely mean that his lordship, being, unhappily, of a somewhat apprehensive temperament, would occasionally get up in the night and prowl about the house. He feared, I suppose, that burglars might have gained access to us.'

'I see. But just how do you come by this information?'

'I have the habit, sir, of occasionally sitting up late in my pantry in order to deal with the household accounts. I have thus heard, if never actually seen, his lordship wandering around.'

'And that happened last night?'

'Certainly not, sir. Had anything of the sort come to my notice last night, I could hardly have failed to communicate the fact to Mr Ringwood when he questioned me this morning.'

'I'd hope not,' Ringwood interjected a shade morosely. 'You told me that everybody had gone to their rooms by eleven.'

'Quite so, Inspector. The entire household appearing to have retired by that hour, and concluding that my services would no longer be required by anyone, I went to bed myself.'

'I see.' Appleby was impressed by the hierarchical distinction made between these two activities. 'Have you any further second thoughts about this whole affair?'

'I fear not, Sir John. But should anything further come to mind, I will communicate it to you at once.'

'Thank you very much, Mr Bagot. And we must not delay you further.'

So Bagot went away – or, as he would have expressed it, withdrew. And Appleby turned to Ringwood.

'We inch forward, wouldn't you say?' he asked. 'We've already had Osprey alarmed by his own shadow – almost literally that – in the library yesterday evening; now we learn that alarm came to him naturally, and that he sometimes prowled Clusters in the small hours as a consequence. It's reasonable to think of him as so employed last night, and as visiting the library in that frame of mind. In something not far short of funk, that is.'

'So we've just got to get Broadwater there, too, at that identical unlikely hour, and what you called a confrontation, Sir John, is in the bag.' Ringwood's tone was sceptical, but his features began to express something else even as he spoke. 'Yes!' he said. 'I believe we're on to it.'

'I think we are. The cardinal point about Broadwater – apparently so absorbed in his fishing – is that he knows he's in a desperate situation. He's been pillaging the Osprey Collection, and trusting wholly to the fact that Osprey is so cagey about it, so near to being a pathological miser, that nobody qualified to detect his depredations is likely to appear. But now suddenly on the scene is this girl Honoria Wimpole, who is a real pro, and shows every sign of getting round the old boy. Moreover, Osprey is – or believes himself to be – hard up, and our American friend Rackstraw is perhaps not the only acquisitive American willing to deal out the dollars and make off with the booty. And there's one other thing.'

'So there is,' Ringwood said. 'Broadwater doesn't even know where the collection is kept. When he had dealings with it Lord Osprey simply trundled it in in that cabinet – or trolley, as Broadwater disparagingly calls it. So, even if his spoils are still at his command, he has no power to restore them unobtrusively to their proper place.'

'At which point, Ringwood, we come to a flaw in the logic – but Broadwater's logic, not ours. For here we have him, not many hours ago, in the library – desperately hunting for the collection's hiding place, although he could do nothing much about it, if he found it. I don't myself judge that to be an impossible mental state. But perhaps it is in his power to make good the most glaring depredations, with some chance of explaining away the minor ones later on.'

'Does it occur to you, Sir John, that, if only he can locate the things, he can stage a burglary of the whole lot?'

'You are absolutely right. And yesterday evening's supposed prowler may have put it into his head to stage such a thing without loss of time. Anyway, here we have Lord Osprey and his brother-in-law, confronting one another in the library. And I rather think that Lord Osprey is armed. You don't have what Bagot calls an apprehensive man prowling a property like this in the middle of the night without a weapon in his hand. A revolver, one imagines.'

'One imagines just that.'

'And next there is a kind of moment of truth. Broadwater loses his cool, and blusters. He says that the situation is intolerable, and that the secret of the collection's hiding place must be confided to him. Hasn't there actually been a thief scouting round that very evening? That sort of thing. There are a few increasingly angry exchanges, and then – for let us be thoroughly dramatic, Ringwood – the scales fall from Lord Osprey's eyes. He realizes that his brother-in-law is a crook; is himself proposing to thieve the whole collection and put the blame on a burglar. Something like that.'

'Just what happens then, Sir John?'

'I don't really know – and you don't, either.' Appleby had calmed down. 'We don't know, that's to say, the stages by which the calamitous situation developed. But here are two frightened men. Osprey's fright turns to panic. He remembers that the key to that *trompe-l'œil* door is in his pocket, and he takes it out and hurls it into the saving darkness at the other end of the library. Broadwater perhaps makes nothing of this gesture, or he may misinterpret it as initiating some sort of attack. He himself produces some threatening gesture, and Lord Osprey points that revolver at him. Broadwater panics in his turn, snatches that weapon from the trophy, and within seconds his brother-in-law is a dead man.'

'And then?'

'I won't say that sanity returns to Broadwater, but I will say that cunning takes control. He cleanses the weapon and returns it to the trophy. He remembers the false alarm, as it had been declared to be, earlier in the evening. He steals out of the house, taking Osprey's revolver with him. Out on the causeway, he chucks the revolver into the moat, and hurries to the little boat-shed. He launches the skiff, paddles it around for a few minutes to get it thoroughly wet, and then gets it back in the shed again, and himself returns to the house. And this false and watery trail having been laid, I suppose he goes to bed – or, as Bagot puts it, retires.'

Detective-Inspector Ringwood had listened to this exposition with gloom.

'It's nine parts speculation,' he said, 'and one part dead certainty. We know that Broadwater killed his brother-in-law, and we conjecture how it happened. In fact, we're sketching what the French police used to be so fond of: a reconstruction of the crime. Do you see any way ahead, Sir John?'

'You can certainly make a summary arrest, Ringwood, and get a warrant from a magistrate which will take him before a bench of magistrates who will almost certainly commit him to the jurisdiction of a Crown

Court. The fun will begin there. And what a judge and jury will make of what we've just been dreaming up, I don't at all know.'

'And that's a fact,' Ringwood said. 'There's no escaping it.'

23

It was a couple of hours later. Bagot's collation had been consumed and the guests had departed. Outside, dusk was giving way to darkness, there was a fitful moon behind slowly drifting clouds; occasionally an owl hooted; a child – but certainly not an adult – might have heard now and then the squeak of a bat. Viewed from a balloon, Clusters would have loomed up as an impressive pile rather than an architectural curiosity.

Appleby, Ringwood and the new Lord Osprey were alone in the marble-sheathed hall. Although each was standing at a comfortable remove from the other, they could all three look straight through one of the enormous windows that gave upon the courtyard, the causeway, and the shadowy ground beyond.

'What's the manpower position?' Adrian Osprey asked. 'A lot of your people have packed up and been sent away.'

'A couple of constables still in the house,'

Ringwood replied. 'And, out there, a couple more with a van. All ready for action at a moment's notice.'

Adrian said nothing further. He had, indeed, been largely silent since being taken into the confidence of the police. He had made no reference to what must be over-poweringly in his mind: the shock that would be felt by his mother when the facts of the situation were revealed to her. But to Appleby and Ringwood he was undeviatingly polite. It had come to him that he was now their host, after all.

'Does anybody go on fly-fishing to this hour?' Ringwood asked. Ringwood had become a shade nervous, and occasionally betrayed the fact. 'Can he have tumbled to the state of play, and made a bolt for it?'

'I don't think so,' Appleby said. 'He had sandwiches with him – and a flask of brandy. Of course he may well suspect he's in a tight place, and be taking his time on the way back to Clusters.'

'We can't be quite sure he isn't armed,' Ringwood muttered. 'He mayn't have chucked away that revolver we're crediting his victim with. It would be natural enough for him to hold on to it, thinking it might be useful.'

'What about this side of the fence?' Adrian asked suddenly. 'Is there a single firearm among the lot of us?'

'Certainly not among the police,' Ringwood snapped. 'Such things aren't issued at all readily. I suppose, my lord, that you could raise a shotgun from somewhere in the house, if you wanted to.'

'It would be a bit thick,' Adrian said. And he added as if to clarify this obscure remark: 'The bastard's my uncle, after all.'

There was silence again for quite a time, and then Appleby spoke quietly.

'Here he is,' Appleby said.

Marcus Broadwater had indeed appeared on the causeway, his rod over one shoulder and his creel depending from the other. But, even as the three men at the window watched, his progress revealed itself as uncertain, as almost stumbling.

'It isn't all that dark,' Ringwood said. 'What's the matter with him?'

'The brandy,' Appleby replied dryly.

It was true that Broadwater had begun to stagger like a drunken man – now near to one and now to the other verge of the causeway. And then, almost instantly, a further explanation of his uncertain progress appeared. With his free arm he was gesturing violently in air, and dark shadows were flitting and darting round his head. The sinister shapes, the momentarily inexplicable congregation of aggressors, grew. Broadwater had thrown down his rod and had both arms in air, his hands vainly attempting some defence of himself.

'The bats,' Adrian said softly. 'Scores of them. But they can't do him any harm – and why are they interested in him, anyway?'

'The dry-fly in his deerstalker hat.' It had come to Appleby instantly. 'The creatures hope to make a meal of them… Good God! Outside – all of us! Ringwood, whistle up your men!'

There was very adequate cause for these sudden shouts on the part of Sir John Appleby. Marcus Broadwater, staggering yet more wildly than before, and with the bats still assailing him at every angle, had gone over the edge of the causeway and into the moat. He was quite dead when they fished him up. Not exactly drowned, the doctor was to affirm. Rather, suffocated in mud. As Adrian might have said, it was a bit thick.